The Secret of
Cravenhill
Castle

THE
NICKI
HOLLAND
MYSTERIES

8

ANGELA ELWELL HUNT

THOMAS NELSON PUBLISHERS
Nashville

Published in Nashville, Tennessee, by Thomas Nelson, Inc., Publishers, and distributed in Canada by Word Communications, Ltd., Richmond, British Columbia, and in the United Kingdom by Word (UK), Ltd., Milton Keynes, England.

Scripture quotation is from the HOLY BIBLE, NEW INTERNATIONAL VERSION ®, Copyright © 1973, 1978, 1984 by International Bible Society. Used by permission of Zondervan Bible Publishing House. All rights reserved.

The "NIV" and "New International Version" trademarks are registered in the United States Patent and Trademark Office by International Bible Society. Use of either trademark requires the permission of International Bible Society.

Library of Congress Cataloging-in-Publication Data

Hunt, Angela Elwell, 1957–
    The secret of Cravenhill Castle / Angela Elwell Hunt.
       p. cm. — (Nicki Holland mysteries : 8)
    Summary: Nicki and her friends travel to Ireland where they find themselves searching for a legendary treasure that will make it possible for their hosts to keep Cravenhill Castle.
    ISBN 0-8407-6305-0 (pb)
    [1. Mystery and detective stories. 2. Buried treasure—Fiction. 3. Ireland—Fiction.] I. Title. II. Series: Hunt, Angela Elwell, 1957– Nicki Holland mysteries : 8.
PZ7.H9115Se 1993
[Fic]—dc20   93-11181
                                                  CIP
                                                  AC

Printed in the United States of America

1 2 3 4 5 6 7 - 98 97 96 95 94 93

Dedication
For Belinda Wilkerson Brown

I waited patiently for the LORD;
  he turned to me and heard my cry.
He lifted me out of the slimy pit,
  out of the mud and mire;
  he set my feet on a rock
  and gave me a firm place to stand.
He put a new song in my mouth,
  a hymn of praise to our God.
Many will see and fear
  and put their trust in the LORD.

—Psalm 40:1–3 (NIV)

Laura

Kim

Nicki

Christine   **Meredith**

W e're going *where*?" Christine Kelshaw asked, her green eyes sparkling as the late afternoon sunshine spilled into the London hotel room.

"We're going to *Ireland*," Nicki Holland answered, sinking onto one of the beds. "Laura's mom met an Irish lady while we were at Buckingham Palace, and they talked all afternoon, and the lady invited us to spend a few days in her castle."

"Isn't it romantic?" Laura Cushman squealed, hugging Gooch, the stuffed animal she had brought all the way from Florida to London. "What a way to end our trip! First we helped catch an international jewel thief—"

"An almost-thief," Meredith Dixon corrected her, wagging her index finger like a scolding schoolteacher. "The crook didn't get away, thanks to Nicki."

"I didn't do anything so spectacular," Nicki answered, thinking of the last mystery the girls had solved, *The Case of the Birthday Bracelet.* "And I couldn't have done anything without all of you."

"Anyway," Laura went on, anxious to tell her news, "my mom said we could fly out of London tomorrow, then we have to take a train and a boat to get to this lady's castle. We'll have three days there before we have to head home and go back to school. Doesn't it sound great?"

"Home sounds great, too," Kim Park said, her soft voice echoing in the room. "I miss my mother and father."

"Just three more days, Kimmie," Meredith said, playfully ruffling Kim's dark hair. "Then you'll have all kinds of interesting stories to tell your parents."

"There's one other important thing," Laura told the girls. Her eyes twinkled. "This Irish lady has a son about our age. And Mom says he's *cute!*"

"Too much!" Christine squealed, covering her face with her pillow. She thrust it off again with a shove, and grinned at the girls. "What are we waiting for? Let's get packed! I want to meet this Irish guy and see his castle!"

Mrs. Virginia Louise Cushman arranged for their flight to Dublin, and early the next morning Nicki and her friends said goodbye to the friends they had made in London and piled their suitcases into a cab headed for Heathrow Airport. "We're meeting Mrs. Shea and her son at the airport," Mrs. Cushman said, her south Georgia accent sounding strangely out of place in the hustle and bustle of London. "You'll like them, girls. She's a charming lady, and her son is just darlin'!"

As the cab pulled away from the curb, Nicki asked Mrs. Cushman how she met Mrs. Shea.

"I met her at the reception we had with the Queen," Mrs. Cushman answered, her beautiful hands delicately gesturing with every word. "She mentioned something about being in town on business—something to do with art or antiquities. Anyway, when she found out we were from the United States, and when she heard that you girls had stopped that terrible thief, she extended the invitation to visit and I accepted for all of us." Mrs. Cushman smiled. "I know you'll like her, girls, and Christine, you'll adore her son. His hair is even redder than yours."

Christine made a face, but Mrs. Cushman didn't notice. "I believe he's about your age," she added, "and he's as cute as a bug's ear."

"Could one really say that a bug's ear is cute?" Meredith asked, her forehead wrinkling in thought.

"Now you've done it, Mama," Laura sighed. "You've flipped the switch in Meredith's brain. Now we'll have to hear about insect anatomy all the way to Ireland."

Mrs. Erin Shea didn't look much older than Nicki's mom, and her auburn hair shone under the airport lights as she nodded to the girls in a firm and friendly greeting. Her brown eyes were sharp as she glanced at her new traveling companions, but her smile was quick and pleasant. As Mrs. Shea introduced herself, Nicki was fascinated by the lady's voice. She could listen to Mrs. Shea's lilting Irish accent all day and never get tired of it.

"Now the lad with me," Mrs. Shea was saying, "is none other than me son, Trant. 'Tis our pleasure and privilege to have you travel with us to our home. It's not often that we get Americans out to Cravenhill Island."

Trant Shea was tall and thin like his mother, but while she stood elegantly slim and erect, he slumped and shifted his weight uncomfortably as the girls turned to look at him. His arms, stuffed awkwardly into the pockets of his jeans, seemed too long for his body, and his red hair and freckles drew attention to his embarrassment.

Then he looked up, and Nicki was startled by his blue eyes. Pale and piercing, they glanced from Nicki to Christine to Laura to Meredith before coming to rest upon Kim, who lowered her eyes and blushed in response to his gaze.

As they made their way to the airport gate, Laura drew Nicki away from the others.

"So, what do you think?" she asked, coyly tilting her head in Trant's direction.

"He's okay," Nicki answered, smiling carefully, "but not really my type."

"He's not mine, either," Laura said. "So at least the two of us won't be fighting over him during our last three days together."

"Honestly, Laura, there's more to life than having a constant boyfriend," Nicki answered, pulling Laura back into the group with the others. "Why can't we just be friendly to the guy?"

Nicki forced herself to concentrate on what Mrs. Shea was saying. "It's British Airways we're taking to Ireland," Erin Shea told Mrs. Cushman. "It's the best airline to fly, absolutely the best. Leather seats, wonderful service—you'll see what I mean in a moment. Here we are—our gate."

"I love her accent," Kim whispered to Nicki as they stood in line to show their boarding passes to the airline attendant. "And I really like her son. Don't you think he's interesting?"

Nicki raised an eyebrow. "Sure, he's interesting," she answered, looking carefully at Kim. "Why don't you find out what he's like and let us know? We can't all talk to him at once." She giggled. "We'd scare him off for sure."

Kim smiled shyly and the dimple in her cheek deepened. "Okay, I'll sit with him," she offered, "and find out what he's like."

Kim and Trant sat together on the plane, Mrs. Cushman took a seat next to Mrs. Shea, and Nicki, Meredith, Laura, and Christine found themselves sitting in a row behind all the others. "Well, Miss Genius," Laura asked, turning to Meredith, "what can you tell us about Ireland? I know you never go anywhere without reading about it first."

Meredith shrugged. "I haven't had much time to learn about Ireland," she answered, "but I can tell you that Ireland is an island west of Great Britain. It is divided politically into Northern Ireland and the Republic of Ireland, and it's often called the 'emerald isle' because of its brilliant green grass. The country's longest river is the Shannon, the land is dotted with lakes—"

"What about Ireland's history?" Nicki asked. "Every corner of London was hundreds of years old and meant something. Is Ireland like that too?"

"In some ways," Meredith answered. "Celtic tribes settled Ireland, then Vikings invaded the area until the Irish king, Brian Boru, broke their strength in 1014. In the twelfth century, England took over Ireland and the Irish kings gradually lost their power. It was a rough time in Ireland's history."

"Well, I'm glad that's all over," Christine said, settling back into her seat and closing her eyes. "We've got nothing to do for the next three days but see the sights and relax. Can't we forget about history and stuff for just a little while? I feel like I'm in school already, and it's still summertime."

Meredith turned her face away and looked out the window. "Okay, I won't say anything else," she said crossly. "But if you need to know anything, go to a library. Don't come looking for me."

Nicki sighed and eased her seat back to a more comfortable position. Tempers had grown short lately, and she hoped her friends wouldn't be at each other's throats for the next three days. Maybe it was time they headed back home so things could get back to normal.

2

The jet landed precisely on schedule in Dublin, and Nicki and her friends found themselves first in a taxi, then aboard a train. "We take the train to Dingle," Mrs. Shea explained as they boarded the train, "and there we board the ferry for Cravenhill Island. We'll be home in about three hours."

"Dingle?" Christine asked, crinkling her nose. "Isn't that an Australian dog?"

"Those are dingoes," Meredith corrected her. "Dingle is a little town on Ireland's southwestern coast between Castlegregory and Cahirciveen."

"At least Dingle is easier to pronounce than those other two," Nicki said, catching Trant's eye. She smiled. "Anyway, I like the train. We can go to the dining car and all sit together at a table and talk."

She led the way to the dining car, where they found a large booth. Nicki slid in next to the window, and Laura and Meredith scooted in beside her. Across from her, Christine took a seat, then Kim slid down the bench. Trant stood awkwardly in the aisle for a moment, then he perched on the edge of the bench next to Kim.

"I've never really known American girls," Trant said, crossing his arms over his chest, "and I'm a bit confused as to what we're supposed to talk about. I like talking, that's no secret at home, and Molly's always telling me to hush me mouth or some such thing. So, let me know what you want to know, and we'll be off with it. Kim here has told me all about you, so I guess I should be a proper host and tell you about Cravenhill, shouldn't I now?"

Nicki grinned at Kim. This new friend of hers was definitely different!

"What's Cravenhill?" Christine asked.

"Me home, the castle," Trant answered. "Haven't you heard of it? Of course not, I'm an idiot for thinking so. Cravenhill Castle has been the home of John Shea since 1502. I'm the fourteenth John Shea, me father the thirteenth, and me grandfather, God rest 'im, was the twelfth."

"Your name is Trant," Laura pointed out. "So how can you be John Shea?"

"I'm John Trant Shea," he answered, lifting his chin proudly. "It was confusing, with grandfather being John, and me dad being Johnny. There was nothing else to call me but Trant, and the name stuck, though I suppose I'll be John by and by."

"Is Cravenhill really a castle?" Christine asked. "With towers and turrets and moats and stuff like that?"

Trant gave Christine a look of mild indignation. "It's a castle proper enough, but there is no moat, nor any need for one. Cravenhill is surrounded by the sea on all sides. Cravenhill Island is barely big enough for the castle, the grounds, the fields, and James's cottage."

"Would you happen to have stables?" Laura asked, leaning forward eagerly. "Do you have horses? I love horses!"

Trant's blue eyes blinked. "We used to have horses," he said. "Once Cravenhill had a mighty company of horses, but none are left."

Trant blinked again nervously, and Nicki wondered why the talk of horses made him so uncomfortable. "What happened to the horses?" she asked gently.

Trant looked away in embarrassment, then turned his head back toward the girls. "Ah, sure, I might as well tell you the truth," he said. "Me father, Johnny Shea, was born the thirteenth John Shea, and Cravenhill's had a run of bad luck ever since. Times have been hard, crops have failed, and now that me grandfather's died, there's no money to pay the estate taxes. We took all the horses to the Dingle auction, and there's talk of selling the art and even the furniture."

"It's a common situation," Meredith said, nodding seriously. "A lot of owners of old estates in England have had to sell paintings, rugs, furniture, and even land just to pay the taxes. Those big places are too expensive to maintain." Meredith eyed Trant steadily. "But surely you don't believe your troubles have come just because your dad is the thirteenth John Shea? That's just plain superstitious."

"And what Irishman is not superstitious?" Trant answered, rearing back in his seat. He paused a moment and leaned in closer to the girls. "Don't tell me mum I told you," he said, lowering his voice, "but that's why we were in London. She took a catalog of our family paintings to art collectors to see if any of them are interested in putting a bit of a bid on the lot of them."

"Did she have any luck?" Nicki asked quietly. "Are you going to be able to raise the money you need?"

Trant shrugged. "'Tis hard to say. Several collectors said they'd be in touch. But only time will tell what becomes of Cravenhill. We have only till the end of the month to find the money we need to pay the estate taxes from grandfather's death. After that—" He shrugged.

"Me parents don't think I know about these things, but I do."

Trant leaned forward and lowered his voice. "If they don't raise nearly forty thousand pounds by the end of the month, Cravenhill Castle goes on the auction block, and we go out the door. I'll be the first John Shea in nearly five hundred years who won't be master of Cravenhill."

"That's terrible!" Laura gasped.

"It sounds like your family needs some sort of plan to raise money," Meredith said, tapping the side of her forehead as she thought. "Maybe we can help."

"It's not actual money we need; we need our treasure," Trant answered, his face settling under a cloud of gloom.

"Your treasure?" Nicki asked. "Why don't you use it? If you've got treasure, why sell off paintings and horses and—"

"Ah, sure, but that's the problem," Trant interrupted. "It's the Cravenhill Curse and me father's bad luck. We have a fortune in treasure to our name, and we don't know where it is. John Shea and his descendants have searched for nearly five hundred years, and no one has found the buried treasure."

"Let me get this straight," Nicki said, putting her palms down on the table in front of her. "Your family knows for sure that there's a treasure somewhere in the castle?"

"On the island," Trant corrected her. "We know the treasure is on the island."

"And no one has found it?" Laura asked. "Has anyone looked?"

Trant gave her a slow smile. "Sure, why wouldn't we look and search and dig?" he asked. "The first and second and third and fourth and fifth John Sheas looked till their dying days, but no sign of the treasure could be found. Who's to say that me father will find it?"

"You really believe there's treasure on the island?" Nicki asked, her mind spinning. She looked at her friends and her eyes gleamed.

"I know what you're thinking," Meredith said, pointing a finger at Nicki. "You want *us* to find the treasure."

"Us? Find treasure that's been hidden for five hundred years?" Christine gasped. "Oh, come on, you don't really think we could."

"We could try," Laura said, her cheeks turning pink. "It'd be fun. Imagine, we could find a cask of diamonds and pearls and rubies—"

"Or we could find nothing," Nicki pointed out. "But it'd be fun to explore the castle while we look." She looked back at Trant. "How about it, Trant? Want to help us look for your family's treasure while we're on your island?"

Trant gazed at them in surprise for a moment, then grinned. "Sure, why wouldn't you be good treasure hunters?" he asked, shrugging. "'Tis a challenge you want, 'tis a challenge you'll get at Cravenhill. Just don't say anything to me mum." He looked quickly toward the compartment where Mrs. Cushman and his mother were seated. "Mum doesn't believe in the treasure," he added. "No one else believes, really. Just me—and Molly O'Hara."

3

Who's Molly O'Hara?" Meredith asked, raising an eyebrow, "and how does she know about the treasure?"

"Molly is our housekeeper," Trant answered, stretching his long legs out into the aisle. "She was born at Cravenhill, and she says if God is willing, she'll die there, too. She knows everything about the place, probably even more than me father, and she's told me about the treasure many times."

"Does she know where it is?" Nicki asked. "Why doesn't she help you get it?"

Trant shook his head. "Either she doesn't know, or she's not saying," he answered. "But I'll get her to tell you the treasure's story herself. Molly's a born storyteller, and the story of Cravenhill is one of her favorites. Trouble is, not many folks today believe the old stories."

"Wait a minute," Meredith interrupted, putting her hand on Trant's. "Is this a true story? We're not going to be out searching for some mythical treasure that doesn't even exist, are we? I'm sure there are better ways to spend our three days."

Trant pressed his lips together and his eyes gleamed defiantly. "I'm not saying anything more," he said finally, his eyes locked on Meredith's. "You'll have to hear the story and see Cravenhill for yourself. Then you can decide whether the place has treasure or not."

Meredith sighed and threw up her hands in a gesture of hopelessness, but Nicki felt a familiar thrill run down her spine. Another mystery! There was something exciting and strange about the story Trant had told them, and staying at Cravenhill Castle had to be more interesting than remaining in London. Still, if they got there and found nothing but an old house on the beach, Meredith was going to be really disappointed. "Why don't we order something to drink," Nicki suggested. "Is anyone else thirsty? My throat is parched."

Nicki picked up the menu on the table in front of her, and Meredith turned around and waved at the waiter who stood at the next table. Suddenly Meredith squealed and her hand grabbed Nicki's with a viselike grip. "Over there," she whispered, turning back to Nicki, her eyes wide with electric excitement. "In that booth behind us. I think that's Professor Jeremy Fulton of Oxford University. He's famous! What in the world is he doing on our train?"

"Going to Dingle, what else?" Christine quipped, snapping her gum as she studied her menu. "Isn't everybody?"

"Who's Professor Jeremy Fulton?" Nicki asked, turning her head quietly to glance at Meredith's celebrity professor. "Why is he famous? I've never heard of him."

"He's the world's absolute best stratigraphologist," Meredith said, turning back to peek at the middle-aged man in the tweed sports coat. "I read in *Scientific American* that he's been making tremendous discoveries about our earth's history and weather patterns by studying rock formations. He's likely to win the Nobel prize for his research someday."

"What's a stra-ti-graph-whatchamacallit?" Laura asked, looking up from her menu.

"Someone who studies historical geology and the interrelationships of layered rocks," Meredith explained, her eyes never leaving the professor. "He's the best."

"That's nice, Meredith, but can we order now?" Christine interrupted. "I wonder if they serve French fries on this train."

"They're called chips here," Nicki reminded Christine. "Maybe you can get an order, if the waiter ever comes over here."

"I'm going to go talk to him," Meredith announced.

"The waiter?" Laura asked.

"No, the professor," Meredith answered. "Don't order any food for me. I'm sure I'll be too busy talking to Professor Fulton to eat."

Meredith stood up, smoothed the wrinkles from her jeans, and fluffed her hair. She gulped and waved at her friends, then walked confidently over to Professor Fulton's table.

"You know," Christine remarked dryly as Meredith left, "she'll probably marry some old guy like that some day. They'll sit around in their lab coats and talk to rats and have kids with the IQs of Einstein."

"Maybe," Nicki answered, peeking over her shoulder again. Meredith had obviously introduced herself; the professor was shaking her hand. "But then again, Meredith just might surprise us one day."

Meredith stayed away through a round of Cokes, double orders of chips, and a trayful of delicious-looking double ice cream sundaes. "I don't know what she sees in that bloke," Trant remarked, spooning the hot fudge sauce off the bottom of his sundae dish. "He looks awfully dry and stodgy to me."

Nicki turned her head to watch Meredith and the professor. The mostly bald Professor Fulton had not given Meredith a polite brush-off, rather his eyes danced as if he were having the time of his life. His neatly trimmed mustache quivered as he whispered and talked, his hands flew through the air, and occasionally he pounded the table in excitement. Meredith sat wide-eyed in front of him, her chin propped on her hands, engrossed in every word.

When she turned back to face the others, Nicki noticed in surprise that Trant and Kim had slipped away.

"Did we lose someone?" she asked Christine and Laura. "Where are Kim and Trant?"

"Haven't you noticed?" Laura said dryly, neatly placing her spoon and napkin on the table. "I never would have imagined them together, but I think we have a new couple in our group. Kim and Trant have been chummy ever since we got off the plane."

"They make a cute couple," Christine said, grinning. "And they say opposites attract. He's tall, she's short, he's got red hair, hers is black, he talks nonstop, she hardly ever says anything. They're perfect for each other."

Nicki laughed. "That's very interesting," she said, peering through the dining car for a glimpse of Kim or Trant. "Who knows what the next few days will bring?"

There was not much time to look around Dingle, for Mrs. Shea led the girls on a quick walk to a boat dock not far from the train station. Though the sun felt warm on her skin, the breeze from the Atlantic chilled Nicki and she wished she had thought to unpack her jacket.

"Hello, Mr. O'Griffin?" Mrs. Shea called, her quick footsteps echoing on the wooden dock. "I've quite a party here to go over to the island. Can you spare a moment to take us home?"

From the tiny boathouse at the end of the dock a tall man appeared. "Ah, sure, it's Erin Shea and company," he said, his rough voice cutting through the gentle lapping sound of the waves as they splashed against the dock and the boats tied there. "So you've decided to come home, have you now? Your husband will be glad to hear it."

"Sure he will," Mrs. Shea answered, smiling patiently. "And since you're so relaxed and casual this afternoon, would you be so good as to ferry us to the island? Eager for the fires of home, I am."

"Doesn't everyone feel that way?" Maurice O'Griffin answered. His tanned face was lined and weather-beaten, and Nicki noticed that even as he made small talk, Mr. O'Griffin's wary eyes raked across the group, watching them all carefully. "Have you picked up lost relatives, Mrs. Shea?"

"No, just friends I've invited for a holiday," Mrs. Shea answered. Maurice O'Griffin turned and headed further down the dock, and Mrs. Shea gestured for the girls to follow her.

"Better take the big boat, Maurice," Trant called, sounding familiar and important. "Sure, if all of us get on the small dingy, there won't be room for the half of us."

"Isn't that a fact," Mr. O'Griffin remarked. He led the way to a large boat, removed his cap, bowed formally from the waist, and waved Mrs. Shea aboard. "Come aboard, lovely ladies, and I'll have you in front of your own fire before you know you've been gone."

4

Oily fumes of diesel fuel filled the air, but the sun stood proudly in the white-blue sky as the boat churned across the water toward the west. Nicki walked over to the bow where Kim and Trant stood staring out to sea. "Is it always this beautiful here?" Nicki asked, holding her face toward the sun. She closed her eyes. "I haven't felt sunshine like this since we left Florida."

Trant laughed. "We've a saying in Ireland—if you don't like the weather, just wait a minute. It'll change. We have sunny days and rainy days, and lots of days in between. Especially on the island the weather is always changing its mind."

Nicki didn't answer, but she opened her eyes to study the water. The Atlantic seemed to be an endless liquid carpet of gray-blue water dancing under the delightful combination of brisk wind and warm sun.

"Look there," Trant said, pointing to the west, and Nicki saw a gray shape looming on the horizon.

"Is that Cravenhill Island?" she asked, squinting to see into the distance.

"The island and a thunderhead," Trant answered. "Ah, sure, we're going to get a bit wet this afternoon."

As they moved closer, Nicki saw the shape more clearly and the sight took her breath away. Far in the distance loomed a rocky island, crowned at its highest point by a gray castle with tall, imposing towers at each end. Above the castle, and even darker gray, hovered a towering rain cloud. As the boat chugged westward, Nicki could see sheets of rain pelting the island and the castle.

"How curious," Nicki said, motioning for Meredith to come closer. "Look at that! It's like the rain begins and ends on the island."

"Professor Fulton said this area has a lot of unusual atmospheric disturbances," Meredith answered, her eyes scanning the sky. "That's why he came to Dingle. He wants to study the weather's effects on geologic formations."

"He should come to Cravenhill Island," Trant answered, a lopsided grin on his face. "We've got the strangest weather in all of Ireland, of that I'm very sure. It will rain in the back of the castle, and not in the front. One winter a cloud covered us with white sticky snow that tasted sweet as candy. Molly gathered it up and made syrup."

"Really?" Kim asked.

Trant nodded. "Ask Molly. She can tell you about that, and more."

"She sounds great," Nicki said, feeling her excitement rise as the castle came more clearly into view. "I can't wait to meet her."

The water beneath the boat became gray-green and gloomy as they neared the thundercloud, and massive black rocks seemed to roar up from the water's edge as they approached Cravenhill Island.

"How are we supposed to get from here to there?" Christine asked, coming over. "That coast is too rocky."

"This is the scenic western approach from the ocean," Trant explained, smiling. "The boat launch is on the eastern side of the island. Ah, sure, rest your minds. Maurice is just showing off a bit bringing us in this way."

Nicki sighed in relief, but as raindrops began to cascade down upon the boat, she and her friends ducked and ran for the cover of the boat's cabin. As Trant had predicted, Maurice O'Griffin appeared to be delighted with the effects of the storm upon his American guests.

"Give you a fright, did I now, ladies?" he asked, smiling broadly. "Not to worry. I'll have you safe in front of your own fire—"

"Soon, please, Mr. O'Griffin," Mrs. Shea interrupted. "My guests are tired and wet. Can we bring the boat in now?"

Maurice O'Griffin grinned, and the gold in his front tooth winked at the girls. "In a flash, ladies, in a flash," he answered, turning the boat toward friendlier waters.

"Isn't it a miracle of grace? Me lady and me boy have come home!"

Nicki looked out from under the sheet of wet newspaper she had been using for an umbrella and saw a solid-looking woman in an apron. The woman's hands were on her hips, and her smile stretched nearly as wide as the large rustic kitchen they had entered. A big calico cat rubbed against her ankles.

"Molly O'Hara?" Nicki whispered to Trant.

Trant nodded as his mother took charge of the situation. "Ladies," Mrs. Shea said, shaking the rain from her umbrella, "meet my housekeeper, Molly. Molly, this is Mrs. Virginia Louise Cushman, her daughter, and her friends. They're Americans, and they'll be staying with us for a few days. Maurice will be bringing up their luggage shortly."

"Well, we're glad to have you," Molly said, her ruddy cheeks gleaming in the weak light from the kitchen windows. "Drop those wet papers on the floor, girls. The devil take him, didn't Maurice O'Griffin have better sense than to drop you out in the rain? If he had waited but a minute or two, the sun would have come out."

"It's all my fault, Molly," Mrs. Shea explained. "I didn't want to wait for the weather. I wanted to get home."

A moment of quiet understanding seemed to pass between the two women as they looked at each other, and when she answered, Molly's voice was soft and quiet. "Aye, there's no place like home, Missy. I'll have tea for you and your guests in a wee bit, so take Mrs. Cushman upstairs and dry yourselves off. Trant, you rascal, go put on dry clothes."

Trant grinned at Molly and took off down a hall, and Mrs. Shea led Mrs. Cushman out of the kitchen to her room. Molly O'Hara turned and smiled at Nicki, Meredith, Laura, Christine, and Kim.

"Now what do I do with the likes of you?" Molly asked, her bright eyes scanning the girls' faces. "What do you want to do first? Eat? Sleep? Change into something warm?"

"How about all of the above?" Christine quipped, shaking the water out of her long wet hair.

"Aye, in proper order," Molly answered, pointing a commanding finger toward the hallway. "First you dry off, then you eat. You can change when Maurice brings your luggage up to the room. March down that hall to the stairs, all of you," she ordered cheerfully. "I'll take you up to your room meself just as soon as I put Mrs. Finnegan out for the night."

"Mrs. Finnegan?" Laura asked, looking around. "We're not taking someone else's room, are we?"

"Mrs. Finnegan is me kitty," Molly answered, scooping up the affectionate cat at her feet. She opened the kitchen door and set Mrs. Finnegan on the back porch. "Off with you, and earn your keep."

Molly closed the door and smiled at the girls. "Off with you now," she commanded, pointing toward the hall.

Molly led them up a narrow staircase to a huge plastered room carpeted with comfortably worn rugs. Wide multi-paned windows on opposite sides of the room flooded the space with light. In the room were three desks, three double beds, and several old chests of dark wood and iron. "What is this place—the barracks?" Meredith asked, looking around. "You could sleep twenty people in here if you had enough beds."

Molly snorted. "It used to sleep many a seafarin' man," she answered, "but now it's any room we want it to be. For this night, 'tis a bedroom. You'll find clean towels in that first trunk, so dry off before you catch pneumonia. Don't you know Maurice O'Griffin is a bloomin' idiot, lettin' you walk through the pourin' rain."

Nicki opened the trunk and lifted out one of the fluffy white towels. As she wrapped her hair in it, she turned to Molly. "Trant says you tell stories," she said, perching on the edge of one of the soft beds. "He said you'd tell us the story of Cravenhill Castle and the treasure. We're supposed to help him find it in the next few days."

Molly drew in her breath when Nicki mentioned the treasure, but then her smile widened in pleasure. "I dinna think you're going to be finding treasure," she answered, shaking her head, "but I'll gladly tell you the story while you dry off."

Molly sat on the bed next to Nicki, and Christine, Laura, Kim, and Meredith came over and sat on the floor in front of her. Molly closed her eyes and took a deep breath: "Long ago, in Dingle, there lived John Shea, and though he worked hard and late, he was a very poor man, don't you know. At last he grew tired of starving at home, so he set out to sea. He was on a ship bound for Lochlin, which is now Denmark, when the captain asked if John cared where he was going. John Shea replied, 'I dinna care much where I go, for I will certainly die of hunger if I stay at home.'"

Molly opened her eyes to make sure the girls were still listening. When she was sure they were, she folded her arms and continued: "When John got to Lochlin, he came to a fine mansion and went in to ask for employment. Inside he found two old men bearded to the waist and one old hag with hair hanging down below her eyes.

"'Where did you come from?' asked one of the old men.

"'What brought you to Lochlin?' asked the other.

"'Well,' John Shea replied, 'to tell the truth, I was starving, and left home to find employment and food.'

"'Sit down,' said one of the old men. 'We will not hurt you, and there is plenty of treasure to be had if there is any good in you.'

"The two old men led John Shea to a room. In the floor of the room lay a flat stone with a ring in the middle. 'Lift this if you can,' one of the old men said. John Shea tried and tried, but he could not lift the ring.

"One of the old men lifted the ring and behold, underneath the stone was a barrel of gold. 'I will give you some of this,' said the old man. So John Shea filled his two pockets. Then the two men asked him if he knew the city of Dingle.

"'Indeed I do,' John answered. 'Don't I go to church there every Sunday, and wasn't I reared in the neighborhood?'

"So the old men told John to go home to Dingle. 'When you are in Dingle, go to the best meat shop in town and buy a leg of mutton,' one of the old men told him. 'Then take a boat to Cravenhill Island and build a good fire outside on the rocks. Roast the mutton, and while the mutton is roasting, the smell of it will come over the place, and at the time of half-light, between night and day, a fairy fort will open.'"

"A fairy fort?" Christine interrupted. "What's a fairy fort?"

"Don't you know anything?" Molly grumbled good-naturedly. "It's where fairies live."

Christine nodded quickly, and Molly resumed her story. "'When the fairy fort opens,' the old man told John Shea, 'a cat will come out of it and come toward you. Hide, for the cat will eat her fill of the mutton, and then lie down before the fire and fall asleep. That is your time. When you have seen the cat sleeping, go inside the fairy fort. In the first room you will find a basin, a towel, and a razor. Take these and bring them to me. Touch nothing else in the fort, for if you do, you may never come out of it alive.'

"Well, John Shea did as he was told. He bought the mutton, made the fire on the island at the time of half-light, and let the cat sleep in peace. He walked into the fairy fort, and saw the basin, towel, and razor. These he picked up. Out of curiosity John walked into the next room, where he saw a treasure beyond all imagining. But he remembered the words of the old man and turned back at once. He took the basin, towel, and razor back to

Lochlin to the old men and the hag.

"'Move up here now, John Shea,' said the old man when John Shea stood before him. 'Lather and shave us.'

"When he had shaved the old men and the hag, he found that they were not old at all, but young twin brothers of eighteen and their sister, a beautiful girl of sixteen. 'Now, John Shea,' the two brothers said to John, 'you have done us much good so we'll take you hunting.'

"Then John Shea remembered the incredible treasure he had found on Cravenhill Island. 'Praise be to God,' he exclaimed, 'I am the happiest man in the world today. I know where the treasure is, and I'll be a rich man now!'

"The two brothers looked at each other and said, 'There was never much power in the Irish of keeping a secret.' Their sister said, 'He is not to be trusted. He would give away the secret.'

"So the brothers and their sister gave John Shea a broth that erased his memory of where the treasure lay. They filled his pockets with gold once more and told him to go his way. Of this adventure, John Shea remembered Cravenhill Island, but he never recalled where the fairy fort and the treasure were to be found.

"With his remaining gold, John Shea built Cravenhill Castle and began the search for his treasure. Today, nearly five hundred years later, John Shea's descendants are still searching."

Molly's eyes widened and wandered toward the window that overlooked the rocky western coast. "On moonlit nights, me thinks I see him out there, searching in the gloom for the fairy fort. I never leave the castle at night. Never."

"What are you afraid of?" Kim asked quietly. "I don't believe in ghosts."

"Ah, but the fairy fort is still there," Molly answered. "I have seen it from my window. And I worry about vengeance from the brothers and their sister, should the treasure be taken from its rightful place."

Molly's voice died away in a whisper, and the room remained eerily silent. Outside, the rain stopped, although a light mist filtered through an open window. Nicki closed her eyes. The tale had seemed so real and *possible* here on this mysterious island, but such things just didn't happen. Fairy forts! Old men who were really young! Hidden gold!

"So that's the legend," Nicki said lightly, opening her eyes. "Well, I guess you're right, it won't make much sense for us to try to find *that* treasure." She forced a pleasant laugh. "Why, I haven't seen a fairy fort in ages."

Molly's eyes were serious. "Sure, and why wouldn't you be doubting my story?" she asked. "But I've seen a fairy fort, and not long ago. And I believe in the treasure—'tis here on the island, I know 'tis."

"You don't really believe that stuff, do you?" Meredith asked, shaking her head. "This *is* the twentieth century."

"Some things never change, do they now?" Molly replied. "I've seen worms fall from heaven, and fairies dance around my stove, but I mustn't ramble on. I'd be here all night long telling you about that!"

5

"**B**ummer, I thought this was going to be a real mystery," Christine said after Molly O'Hara left them. "But Molly is just superstitious, and all that stuff about fairies is crazy. We'd be wasting our time to help Trant look for treasure."

"How does it feel to have a boyfriend who believes in fairies?" Laura asked Kim, a teasing note in her voice.

"Leave her alone," Meredith said, defending Kim. "Maybe there is something to Molly's story. After all, Trant isn't crazy. Maybe this castle was used as a fort or something in a war, or maybe pirates had an outlook here. Maybe there is real treasure, and that story about John Shea and the fairy fort is a legend invented to disguise the truth."

"Then how do we find the *real* truth?" Nicki asked. "That story is all we've got to go on. If there is treasure, it seems to me the only place to start is with the fairy fort."

"Calling all fairies! Come out, come out, wherever you are!" Christine shouted, cupping her hands to her mouth.

"Don't be silly," Laura snapped as Christine dissolved into giggles. "Either we take on this mystery seriously, or we don't waste time on it at all. I say we put it to a vote."

"If we don't work on it, Trant's family won't find

the treasure, and they won't have enough money to pay their taxes," Kim mentioned quietly. "I want to help Trant, no matter what we have to do."

"If we do investigate this mystery, we might find absolutely nothing," Nicki pointed out. "But we'd have a lot of fun exploring this castle and the island. We've got three days, so we might as well do something."

"Okay, let's vote," Laura said. "All in favor of looking for the fairy treasure, raise your right hand."

Nicki raised her hand immediately, and Kim followed. Meredith's hand went up slowly, then Laura shrugged and lifted her hand as well. Christine scowled, then raised her pinky finger. "I still think it's a waste of time," she said, "and this isn't the sort of thing I'm going to mention in my 'what I did this summer report' when we get back to school. But since I'm outvoted, I guess it's okay with me if we go on an elf hunt."

"That's fairy, not elf," Kim corrected. "Elves live with Santa at the North Pole."

Christine rolled her eyes. "Boy, Kim, have you got a lot to learn," she sighed.

After changing into dry clothes, Nicki and her friends came down the long wooden staircase and looked around. The castle was not as large as Nicki had imagined. It actually seemed cozy, with brightly painted plastered walls that bore paintings of stiff-looking men and women in antique clothes. The planks of the wooden floor were dark with age, and the thick, faded carpets scattered through the hallways muffled the girls' timid footsteps as they searched for Mrs. Cushman and Trant.

"I hear them this way," Kim said, tiptoeing down a

long hall. Nicki and the others followed, giggling and gawking at their surroundings.

The hallway ended in a large cheerful room with high ceilings and a comfortable mix of warm leather and bright prints. A welcoming fire crackled in a grand fireplace at the end of the room, and Mrs. Cushman and Trant were sitting on a slightly frayed sofa in front of the fire. Nicki instinctively liked the room with its smell of burning logs, sea air, and polished wood.

Mrs. Shea was standing at a desk in the corner of the room, a radio transmitter in her hand. "Thank you very much," she spoke into the transmitter as she waved and smiled a welcome to the girls.

The radio filled the room with static, then Nicki recognized the rough voice of Maurice O'Griffin. "I'm sorry about this," he said, "but the message was waiting for me when I brought the boat back."

"It's quite all right," Mrs. Shea said, pressing the button on the transmitter. "I understand. It can't be helped, Maurice. We'll talk to you again soon. Over and out."

She turned off the radio and sighed.

"Not bad news, I hope?" Mrs. Cushman asked, lifting a cup of tea to her lips.

"Yes, I'm afraid 'tis," Mrs. Shea answered, taking a seat in a large wing chair by the fire. "That was Maurice O'Griffin. The art dealer from London who was supposed to come this weekend got as far as Dingle, then canceled his visit. I hoped he would come another time, but Mr. O'Griffin says the man seemed reluctant to reschedule."

"Then he is losing out on a rare opportunity," Mrs. Cushman said, smiling. "Someone else will come. Don't worry, you'll sell the paintings you need to sell."

"I'm afraid it's just another example of the Cravenhill Curse," Mrs. Shea sighed. Her eyes were dark as she stirred her tea. "We'll never raise the money for the estate taxes. I wouldn't mind losing the castle so much because I could be happy anywhere. I just hate to see all these beautiful things end up in the hands of the highest bidder. These things are precious to my husband—you're looking at five hundred years of family heritage."

Nicki looked around at the lovely furniture, carpets, and paintings. "Everything is so beautiful," she said, smiling at Mrs. Shea. "And you have so many valuable things—surely you could sell just a couple of paintings and raise the money you need."

Mrs. Shea's smile did not reach her eyes. "I thought so, too, until we began to advertise things for sale. Do you think anyone even came to see them? No one ever responded to a single ad. Sure, we've even advertised to sell the entire estate, and we haven't had one response. Who wants to buy an ancient castle today?"

She shook her head as if shaking off a bad mood. "But I forget my duty as hostess. Come closer, girls, there's biscuits and tea here, strong, sturdy stuff that'll shake the cobwebs out of your head. And no one in the southwest of Ireland can beat Molly O'Hara's biscuits."

Nicki and Christine were the first to reach the tray where Molly had set out an assortment of fresh baked cookies. "I'll never get over calling cookies 'biscuits,'" Christine said, laughing as she selected a huge frosted oatmeal bar. "But I'll never forget eating them!"

"Don't eat too many," Meredith said, selecting a dainty round cookie covered with apricot preserves. "If we're going to begin our investigation, we want you to be light on your feet, Christine."

"And what investigation would that be?" Mrs. Shea asked lightly.

"Nothing to worry about, Mum," Trant answered, standing up. His eyes sought Nicki's and telegraphed a warning message. "We were just on our way out, anyway."

"All right then," Mrs. Shea answered, sinking back into the cushions of her chair. "Just mind yourself, Trant, and don't drag our guests into any of the wild and rocky places. Remember, they're young ladies."

Trant winked at Kim before leading the way out. "It's not likely I'd be forgetting that," he answered.

"Where do you want to go?" Trant asked as he led them out of the drawing room and into another large hall.

A tall suit of armor stood behind Nicki, and she took a moment to admire it before answering Trant. "Where should we begin?" she said. "You know this place better than we do. Where do you know the treasure *isn't?*"

"I really don't believe it's in the house," Trant said, waving his hand to take in the entire castle. "This place has been explored and remodeled and renovated through the years, and if there was gold hidden here, it would have shown up."

"If the treasure was inside the castle, it wouldn't fit the legend," Meredith pointed out. "In the legend, John Shea saw the treasure before he even thought about building the castle. Unless he happened to build the castle right on top of the treasure, it can't be inside. It has to be somewhere outside."

Nicki walked over to the heavy wooden door at the end of the entry hall. "So what's outside?" she said, tugging on the iron ring to open the door. The door groaned, then opened with a long, protesting squeak. Through the opening Nicki could see the blue expanse of the ocean and the dark rocks that rimmed Cravenhill Island.

"Not much," Trant answered simply. "On this western side, the island is rocky and rough. The eastern side, though, is protected from the sea winds and it's really nice. James has planted gardens, and there's a nice lawn. The fields are south of the castle."

"Who's James?" Christine asked, her gum snapping noisily in the quiet of the hall.

"Our grounds keeper," Trant answered. "James Murray. He's worked here for years. I can't remember a time when James wasn't around."

Nicki shrugged. "Would he mind if we talked to him? Maybe he'll know something about the treasure."

"Or about fairies," Kim inserted. "If Molly has seen them, maybe James has, too."

"I doubt that," Laura remarked dryly. "One lulu in the castle is enough."

Nicki nodded to Trant. "We'd like to meet James," she said. "Will you take us to him?"

"Sure," Trant answered, closing the rough door Nicki had opened. He shrugged as he turned to face them again. "We never use that door," he said. "It's too noisy and too heavy. Everyone comes and goes through Molly's kitchen."

6

The difference in the views from the front door and Molly's kitchen door was as dramatic as the movie scene in which Dorothy goes from black-and-white Kansas to colorful Oz. Nicki hadn't seen much of the gardens in her rain-drenched run from the boat launch to the castle, but now the sun was shining and Cravenhill Castle's velvet lawn and gardens shimmered in emerald beauty. Tall flowers waved their pink and purple heads as they lined the brick-paved walk, and boughs of the green oaks gently swayed in the sea breeze. Under the trees, a dark green carpet of English ivy covered the ground. Birds twittered from someplace unseen as the young people approached.

"This is beautiful," Nicki breathed, twirling around in the late afternoon sun. "Like the Garden of Eden."

"It's all right," Trant agreed modestly. He led the way down one of the garden pathways, and Nicki and the girls followed. "When I was a little lad, I used to play out here in the gardens and pretend I was Robin Hood. James was my one and only merry man, but he stayed with me for hours while I played."

"Where did you go to school?" Christine asked, taking giant steps to keep up with Trant.

"Me mother taught me for several years," Trant answered. "Then I caught a ride on Maurice O'Griffin's boat and went to school in Dingle. That's where I'll be headed back in a couple of weeks."

An abrupt gust of wind tossed the girls' hair. "Oh, that wind," Laura fussed, smoothing her hair. "Does it blow like this all the time?"

Trant squinted up at the sky. "Another storm's coming up," he answered. "Clouds from the west. It'll be rough on the water soon."

"What was it like taking a boat to school?" Laura asked. "I think it'd be cool!"

"It wasn't always great," Trant answered. "When bad weather blew up, which was pretty often, I had to stay in Dingle with Maurice. Or he wouldn't be able to come out and get me, so I'd miss a day and have to do double work the next."

"Bummer," Christine said, crinkling her freckled nose. "I guess living on an island does have its disadvantages."

"But look at the advantages!" Laura gushed. "Living in a castle with servants—"

"They're not servants," Trant corrected her. "Molly is like one of the family. My parents haven't been able to pay her a salary, so she does sewing on the side for her income. James raises vegetables in the garden patch behind the gardener's cottage. My parents don't pay him, either."

"Then how do your parents make money?" Meredith asked, her dark eyes piercing and direct. "I don't want to embarrass you or anything, but how do you get money for groceries?"

Trant blushed at the directness of her question, but he lifted his chin. "Once a month Maurice O'Griffin brings over paying tourists who tour the castle and the grounds," he said. "They pay five pounds each to walk through the house and have tea in the drawing room. Tourist money saved us when the crops failed. We haven't even bothered planting crops in the south fields for the last two years."

"You live in a tourist attraction?" Laura asked, lifting an eyebrow. "Like Disney World?"

"No," Trant answered, his eyes narrowing. "We wouldn't open the castle at all if we didn't have to. Me father catches fish and sells them, and Mum does what she can, but it's not enough. Maurice O'Griffin would have the paying visitors over here five days a week if we'd let him, but Father won't allow it."

"When we find the treasure, you will not need to have paying visitors," Kim said smoothly, smiling up at Trant. "Everything will be fine."

Suddenly a shadow fell over the group as if a huge hand had passed before the sun. A rumble came spiraling down from the clouds overhead, and the keening wail of the wind brought goosebumps to Nicki's arms. Nicki looked toward Meredith, who opened her mouth in a soundless scream and pointed to something behind Christine.

The group emitted a collective gasp. Coming straight toward them was a radiant ball of what looked like dancing light. Glowing red, orange, and yellow, it advanced along the garden path and paused behind Christine's head, pulling her hair up and out until she looked like a giant pin cushion with wide eyes. Without warning, the light ball darted into the leaves of a nearby oak tree. The wind stopped, there was an instant of absolute silence, and then the tree writhed as if some unseen creature thrashed it in a death grip. Even the air seemed to be holding its breath until the top of the oak tree exploded into a shower of green leaves.

Nicki felt the skin prickle on the back of her neck,

and goose bumps stood out along her arms.

"What was that?" Christine asked, her voice shaky.

"I'm going to faint," Laura gasped, clutching Meredith's hand. "Trant," Nicki said, trying to keep her voice steady, "does this sort of thing happen often around here?"

Trant blinked in astonished silence, but he nodded slowly. "Aye," he said, finally taking his eyes from the tree where the mysterious glowing ball had vanished. "Though I've never seen it till now. If you ask me what it is, I'd say I don't know. But if you were to ask Molly O'Hara, she'd say we just received a powerful warning."

"Warning? From whom?" Meredith asked, her nostrils flaring in indignation.

"From the fairies," Trant replied.

7

W e've got to talk to Molly O'Hara right now," Christine said, her hair still flying in all directions from the effects of the mysterious ball of light. "I felt the weirdest sensation—like my entire body was tingling."

"That's how lightning would make you feel," Meredith said, raising a finger to her lips thoughtfully. "But that was like no lightning I've ever seen."

Raindrops began to fall from the gray sky overhead, sharp as a sword against Nicki's skin. "This way to James's cottage," Trant shouted, motioning for the girls to follow. "It's just behind these trees."

They made it to the safety of the cottage's front porch just before the skies opened in a terrific waterfall. The sudden storm blew foul winds and strangling rain upon the earth, turning what had been immaculate flower beds into pools of black mud. "Good grief, we're lucky we made it here," Christine said, wiping her arm across her nose. "We could have drowned in all this rain."

"It rains like this all the time," Trant answered, grinning. He paused to knock on the cottage door. "I only hope James hasn't been caught out in it."

Trant knocked again, but there was no sound or movement from within the cottage. "He must be out working somewhere," Nicki said, sitting down in one of the wicker rockers on the porch. "Can we just sit here and talk until the rain stops? Maybe James will come along later."

Trant agreed, and the girls settled into the chairs on the porch. Nicki noticed with a quiet smile that Trant and Kim sat together on the wicker love seat.

Christine, Laura, and Meredith made themselves at home on James's porch swing and began swinging energetically. "Okay, about this treasure," Christine shouted, struggling to be heard as the rain pounded against the roof overhead. "Where do we start? If you were serious about that warning from the fairies, maybe the treasure's somewhere in the garden. Maybe it's even near that tree where the ball of light disappeared."

"That was the tallest tree in the area," Kim agreed. "It is probably the oldest, too."

"I'm not really sure I want to believe that light ball was fairies," Nicki said, glancing at Trant. "What do you think?"

Trant shook his head. "The Irish are superstitious, and folks like Molly and even James really believe in fairies," he answered. "I dinna think my mother and father go in for such things, but there are some things I dinna understand yet—"

Trant's voice trailed away, and Nicki saw two men coming toward them down the garden path. They were oblivious to the pouring rain and walked through it easily, as if they were used to being surrounded by water. "James Murray?" she questioned, looking at Trant.

He nodded. "James and me father," he answered. "And I dinna think they are in the best of moods."

Nicki watched as the men grew closer. Deep in conversation, they did not look up toward the cottage as they approached. The taller man was thin like Trant, with dark hair and bushy brows. He gestured emphatically as they walked and talked, and it was clear that he was upset about something.

The other man kept his head down most of the time. He wore a battered wet fishing cap over his hair, and on his face was a thick white beard. He carried a bucket and a fishing rod and reel. Both men wore clothes that were dark and wet, although neither seemed to care.

"I tell you, 'tis a crying shame," Mr. Shea's booming voice reached the girls on the porch as the rain lightened to a drizzle. "We've done all we can, James, and nothing's happening to lift this cursed luck. We've published an advert, called the art dealers, opened the house—"

"Hello there, Dad," Trant called out. "Hello, James."

Mr. Shea raised his head abruptly and closed his mouth. He nodded politely to the girls.

"Dad, these are the girls Mother met in London," Trant said, motioning toward Nicki and the others. "Meet Nicki, Kim, Christine, Meredith, and Laura. Girls, this is me father and James Murray, the fellow I've told you about."

James put down his bucket and took off his fishing hat. "Pleased to meet you, I'm sure," he said.

"Thanks," Nicki answered, speaking for the group. "We were just enjoying your porch to get out of the rain."

"And you're welcome to it," James answered. "I wouldn't be a proper host if I denied lovely ladies a dry porch, would I now?"

Though James Murray smiled politely, Nicki noticed that his mouth was tight, and after a moment he gave Mr. Shea an awkward glance. "We'll talk another time, James," Mr. Shea said, moving away through the trees.

James Murray came forward and placed his bucket on the porch. Inside was an assortment of fish, and Laura turned her head away and held her nose. "Ugh," she said, breathing through her mouth. "What a smell!"

"Ah, girlie, 'tis the smell of nature's bounty," James Murray answered, grinning devilishly. He propped the rod and reel up against a post and took off his wet jacket. "Now why would you be bringing your friends to see me, John Trant Shea?" he asked, winking at Trant. "Could it be that you just wanted to show them the most handsome man in Ireland?"

"Not really," Trant answered, smiling back at James. "But we wanted to ask you some questions, and maybe borrow a shovel. We're going to look for the treasure."

"And what treasure would that be?" James asked, his hands on his hips. His dark eyes darted from Trant to Nicki. "I'll not have you digging up me gardens."

"We won't hurt anything," Nicki answered. "We just wanted to look and see if there's anything to the story of John Shea and the fairy fort."

James Murray's merry eyes darkened. "Why would you modern young folks be searching for such things?" he asked, with a cautionary lift of his hand. "Dinna you know such things aren't possible?"

"There's no harm in looking, is there?" Laura asked timidly. "We won't bother anything."

"You are a bunch of idiots for thinking about it," James answered, forcing a shrug. "But you can borrow my shovels if you like, just be careful to put them back when you're through, eh, Trant?"

"Look, the sun's coming back out!" Christine yelped, pointing to a smudge of sun that dappled through the cloud cover. "The rain's almost gone."

"We're off then," Trant said, leading the girls off the porch. "You're a pack of idiots, don't you know?" James

Murray called as Trant led the way to the toolshed. "You'll be sorry you've wasted your time."

The girls stood with Trant at the base of the tall oak tree. The dark ground underneath their feet was littered with green oak leaves, and as she gazed upward, Nicki thought she could see a dark stain at the top.

"Before we dig anything, maybe we should have a closer look at this tree," Nicki said, looking upward. "Up there, near the top, doesn't it look like the tree's actually *burned*?"

Meredith came to stand near Nicki. "Yes, it does," she agreed, tilting her head back. "Trant, are you any good at climbing trees? Can you go up and check this out?"

"If he won't go, I will," Christine volunteered, laying her hands on the trunk of the tree. "I climb trees with my brothers at home all the time."

Trant scowled at Christine. "I can do it," he muttered, handing his shovel to Kim. He studied the base of the tree. "If you'll give me a boost, I think I can climb all the way up." He hoisted one leg onto a gnarled bump near the ground. "Just lift me high enough so I can get to that next branch."

"I'll give you a boost," Christine offered. She laced her fingers together, braced her legs, bent her knees, and presented her hands to Trant. "Climb up," she said, and Trant slipped his muddy shoe into her hands.

"Gross," Christine grumbled, straining under Trant's weight. "I forgot about the mud."

"That's all right. I've got it," Trant said, pulling himself up. He caught hold of the first branch and sat on it. Once he was secure, he reached for a higher branch, pulled himself up, and soon he was climbing through the branches with ease.

"Be careful, your shoes are muddy," Kim called. "Don't slip!"

"I'm fine," Trant shouted down. He paused for a moment and looked down at the girls. "Sure, and don't you all look like little mice down there?" he joked.

"Don't look down," Meredith warned. "Just get to the top of the tree and tell us what that black mark is."

The remaining leaves nearly blocked the view of Trant as he climbed, and his voice floated eerily down. "It's burned, all right," he called. "Two branches up here are as bald as an egg. Whatever that ball of light was, it scorched this tree."

"Like lightning," Meredith said, pursing her lips thoughtfully. "Just like lightning, but lightning is supposed to reach from the ground to the sky when the negatively charged base of a cloud induces a positive charge in the ground."

"Okay, Miss Encyclopedia, be quiet. Trant's climbing down," Christine said, elbowing Meredith.

"No, go on, I'm interested," Nicki said. "Was this lightning or not?"

"Well, when streams of negative particles from the cloud begin to probe downward, they create a conductive channel only an inch or two wide," Meredith explained. "When the channel reaches the ground—or in this case, a tree—a powerful current zooms up to the sky. The bright flash occurs when the electrical charge excites the molecules of air in its path, causing them to release light."

"So that ball we saw couldn't be lightning," Nicki said slowly, thinking aloud. "Because it wasn't anywhere near the ground. It was just wandering around."

"It reminded me of a cat," Laura said. "Like a little lonely cat that wants to rub itself against someone's legs. It came right up to us, stopped a second, then took off." She giggled nervously. "I guess we scared it off."

Meredith snapped her fingers. "I know! Professor Fulton specializes in weather and rocks. We could go into Dingle and ask him about it. Maybe he can explain it."

"Hey, Trant, could we go into Dingle?" Nicki called up into the tree. Trant was nearly down; there were only about six branches left to maneuver.

"When do you want to go?" he answered, shifting his weight onto the next branch. "Maybe tomorrow, I suppose we could go."

"That'd be nice," Nicki said, turning to Meredith. "We could take the boat over, go see your professor—"

"Look out!" Kim shrieked, her eyes wide with fear. "He's slipping!"

Nicki looked up for an instant and saw Trant teeter on the edge of a branch still twelve feet above their heads. His right foot was firmly planted on the tree limb, but his left foot had slipped from the branch. Off balance, he grabbed for something to steady himself, but missed and clawed the empty space around him as gravity pulled him off the branch.

"Ohmigoodness, help!" Christine wailed, and a thick swallow rose in Nicki's throat and wouldn't go away. She watched in horror as Trant fell soundlessly through the air.

8

There was a sharp and brittle crack of weathered wood, then a sickening thud as Trant landed on the soft dark earth. Nicki held her breath until Trant groaned. "That hurt," he moaned softly, his hand waving helplessly as he lay on the ground. His other arm lay limply by his side.

"Run, Kim and Christine, and get help," Nicki said, kneeling by Trant. "Meredith, help me here. How badly is he hurt?"

"I'm sure the wind has been knocked out of him," Meredith answered, reaching for Trant's wrist. She cocked her head silently for a moment as she felt his wrist, then she smiled at Nicki. "His pulse is good and strong."

"I think he only hit that one branch with his hand on the way down," Nicki said, closing her eyes to block out the memory of Trant's horrific fall. "So unless he hit something hard on the ground—"

"Me leg," Trant moaned. "Me leg is killing me."

Nicki glanced at Trant's right leg and grimaced. She hadn't noticed it at first, but a large stone lay under his calf.

"I think he may have bruised his leg on this rock," Nicki whispered to Meredith. "He may even have broken it."

"I'm going to faint," Laura whispered, her blue-green eyes glittering in her pale face.

"Sit down, then, because we're busy here," Meredith answered coldly, peering into Trant's eyes. "If you think you're going to pass out, lean against a tree."

Laura whimpered softly, but she didn't say anything else as Meredith and Nicki made Trant as comfortable as possible without moving him. "There's nothing more we can do," Meredith said finally, wiping a smudge of dirt from Trant's pale cheek. "I'm afraid to move him. If we try, and he's broken a rib or something, we could puncture a lung."

The sound of feet pounding over the grass finally reached the girls, and Nicki felt a flood of relief sweep over her. Trant's father led the crowd running down the garden path, and Mrs. Cushman, Molly O'Hara, and Kim followed behind him.

"It's all right, Trant," Mr. Shea said gruffly as he knelt beside his son. "Your mother has radioed for Maurice O'Griffin's boat, and we'll have you to the doctor directly."

A moment later Christine and James Murray ran from the direction of the gardener's cottage. James was carrying a long pole wrapped in canvas, and it took Nicki a moment before she realized he was carrying a stretcher.

"Thank you girls, you've done enough," Mr. Shea said, glancing at Nicki and Meredith for only an instant before returning his attention to his son. He nodded grimly at James. "You lift his shoulders, James, and I'll lift his legs onto the stretcher."

James spread the stretcher out onto the ground next to Trant, and Nicki and Meredith stepped out of the way. When his father's hands were under his shoulders, Trant's eyelids fluttered weakly. "I'm sorry," he whispered, moaning. "Sorry, Dad."

Mr. Shea's smile was bitter. "And why should you be worrying about this, son?" he asked. "'Tis my bad luck, the thirteenth John Shea. Don't you be worrying your head about anything."

Trant didn't answer, and Mr. Shea and James Murray quickly moved Trant onto the stretcher and then lifted the stretcher from the ground. Laura opened her mouth to say something, but Meredith silenced her with a stern look. "Just be quiet, Laura," Meredith warned. "If you're going to faint, put your head between your knees."

Laura clamped her mouth shut in a pout and crossed her arms.

When Mr. Shea and James Murray were well up the garden path, Molly O'Hara turned to the girls, her hands firmly planted on her hips. "Now I wouldn't be asking you this, but I've a right to know," she said, her cheeks flushed even redder than usual. "What in heaven's name was me boy doing up in that tree?"

"It's a long story," Nicki began, fidgeting nervously under Molly's unrelenting gaze. "But earlier today, before the rain, we saw this ball of light go up the tree. We came back to investigate, and Trant was climbing down—"

"Saints preserve us!" Molly said, throwing up her hands in horror. "You saw the fairy ball! And all these years I thought I was the only one seein' such things!"

"You've seen it, too?" Meredith asked. "When? Where?"

Molly pressed her lips together firmly and shook her head. "Don't you know there's no use in talking about such things?" she asked, thrusting her hands stubbornly into her apron pockets. "You see what harm comes from messin' with the fairies? You should leave them alone, and they won't bother you. Just leave them alone, girls, and remember that Molly O'Hara has given you fair warning!"

She turned and panted up the path after the others, and Nicki looked at her friends. "I don't know what we should do now," she admitted, feeling a little sick. "It'll be dark soon, and everyone will be busy taking care of Trant."

"Let's do just one thing," Meredith said, tilting her head to one side. "Before we go in, let's take a walk around the island on the beach. I'd like to get a clearer picture of exactly where we are."

Christine made a face. "We're in the middle of Creepsville," she answered. "Time Warp Central. Never Never Land."

"I think a walk would be nice," Laura volunteered. "I know they don't want us underfoot back in the castle. The Sheas may even think that Trant's accident was our fault."

"I don't think so," Kim answered. "Mrs. Shea was very frightened when I told her the news, but she was calm, too. She said, 'Boys will be boys,' and then she went straight to the radio to call for a doctor and Mr. O'Griffin's boat."

"If only Molly O'Hara will forgive us," Christine said, rolling her eyes. "If she doesn't, we'd better pray she doesn't send the fairy goon squad after us."

The sea was a constant presence on the island, and when they walked down from the garden to the quiet beach on the eastern side of the island, Nicki realized how calming the constant sound of the waves could be. Here on the eastern shore the quiet waves shimmered in the light from the setting sun and rippled gently toward the shoreline. A few feet up from the sandy beach the lush green of James's gardens rose like rich embroidery on a lady's shawl.

"See that light out there?" Meredith said, pointing toward the watery horizon. "I think that's O'Griffin's boat coming in. We'd better get out of his way if he's coming to get Trant."

"I agree," Nicki said, and they quickened their pace and walked north along the beach. High on the hill, tiny lights in the castle were beginning to gleam through the gathering dusk. "It's so peaceful here," Nicki said, watching their long shadows on the water as they walked. "Like Florida in many ways, but very different."

"I'll say it's different," Christine muttered. "When's the last time a fairy came up to you at home and nearly bit your head off?"

Nicki didn't answer, but walked faster, and the pleasant peace of the eastern shore faded. It was almost as though a line existed where green stopped and bleak began, and the girls soon found themselves on the western shore of the island where black rocks ringed the beach and the wind blew strong and stiff from the Atlantic Ocean. Here was the smell of low tide and crawling things, and Nicki began to wish she had brought her flashlight. It was nearly dark, and only one light shone from the castle on this side—a strong, bright light from an upper tower.

"Do you suppose that light is to warn sailors?" Laura asked, wrapping her thin sweater closer around her. "What if a boat crashed on these rocks?"

"Maybe that has something to do with the treasure," Meredith said thoughtfully, carefully skirting the waves that broke near her feet. "Maybe a boat did crash here once, maybe John Shea knew about it, and when there were no survivors he found the ship's treasure and buried it somewhere on the island. He had to wait for time to pass, you see, so people wouldn't be suspicious about his sudden wealth. Maybe he even left Cravenhill, and when he came back he couldn't remember where he had hidden the treasure."

"So he built his castle here and waited for his memory to come back?" Kim asked.

"That's not a bad theory," Nicki said. "If he did find treasure, that would explain how he got the money to build the castle in the first place."

"So if he buried the treasure and couldn't remember where it was, it must have been a really inconspicuous spot," Meredith added.

"What kind of spot?" Christine asked, crinkling her nose.

"It was a place that looked like lots of other places," Meredith explained. "If it was a unique place, surely he would have remembered it."

"Like under a rock," Nicki said, stopping in the sand. She looked upward to the towering black rocks above the beach.

Meredith followed Nicki's thoughts. "Beneath those rocks would be a good place," she said. "This sand under our feet is covered with water at high tide—remember how it was when we came in this afternoon? You could dig beneath those rocks only at low tide."

Nicki whistled. "When's low tide tomorrow, Meredith?" she asked. "We could get a shovel and dig out here and no one would even notice."

"Early in the morning, probably six o'clock," Meredith answered, her eyes brightening with enthusiasm.

"Bummer," Christine remarked. "Too early for me."

"Stay in bed then," Nicki answered. She couldn't help grinning. "Tomorrow morning we dig for buried treasure!"

9

The gentle hum of Nicki's travel alarm clock woke her, and she automatically reached to silence it. As she lay in bed, the haze of sleep lifted gradually from her brain, but it disappeared altogether when a hand reached out and touched her shoulder.

Nicki's eyes flew open. Kim was already dressed and sitting on the edge of the bed. "Are we still going out to the beach?" Kim asked, her eyes gleaming in the semi-darkness of the room. "It's nearly six o'clock."

"Yes," Nicki answered, struggling to sit up under the weight of Molly's heavy comforter. "What are you doing up already?"

"I couldn't sleep," Kim answered. "I was worried about Trant. Even though Mrs. Shea told us he was okay and the doctor was only keeping him in the hospital overnight for observation, I'm worried about him."

"He'll be okay," Nicki said, swinging her feet onto the cold wooden floor. "A broken leg isn't the end of the world. I'm just glad he didn't break any ribs."

Christine popped up like a jack-in-the-box and pushed her hair from her face. "Is it time?" she asked, wide awake. "What should we wear? I've never been on a treasure dig before."

"Just wear jeans and a sweatshirt," Nicki said, padding over to wake Meredith and Laura. "Anything grubby. It's going to be messy out there."

Christine hopped out of bed and crossed to the western window. Pushing a glass panel open, she stared outward and sniffed the air. "It's really spooky out there," she reported. "The sun's not up yet, and it smells like rain."

"Rain will not hurt us," Kim replied, opening her suitcase. She pulled out a water-repellent jacket and tied it around her shoulders. "This is important for Trant and his family."

"Let's be quiet as we leave the castle," Nicki said, digging through her suitcase for her jeans. "Mr. and Mrs. Shea were up late last night taking Trant to Dingle, and they won't be happy if we wake them."

Nicki remembered to exit through Molly's quiet kitchen door, and she led the girls through the darkness to the toolshed where they had left their shovels. "Three shovels, a pick axe, and a hoe," she said, shining her pocket flashlight over the contents of the shed. "Let's take whatever we can use. The more holes we dig, the more likely we are to find John Shea's treasure."

The girls each took a tool, and Nicki led them down the quiet garden path to the gloom of the castle's western side. The difference in the two beaches was remarkable, Nicki thought. The green eastern castle yard was already beginning to feel the warmth of the rising sun, but on the western beach the landscape still loomed cold and dreary. Fog covered the beach, and its cold, ghostly mists floated aimlessly over the strip of land where rough breakers crashed. But low tide had carried the waters far from the sentinel row of black rocks, and Nicki and her friends could walk on the sand along the base of the cliff.

"Meredith, why don't you and Laura dig under this first rock," Nicki suggested. "Chris, you and Kim dig under that second big rock there, and I'll start digging under the third."

Meredith shivered in the cold, but she nodded, and Laura stopped her teeth from chattering long enough to complain that the wind was too cold for work. But Laura picked up the hoe and began chopping away at the wet sand, and Nicki grabbed a shovel and walked further down the beach to the third massive rock.

She felt the shovel bite into the wet earth, but the cushioning silence of the clammy fog that swirled around her ankles muffled the sound. A sudden shiver gripped Nicki, and she grasped the handle of her shovel more firmly. She felt as though she was alone in the dark, with only the bawling winds at her side. The wild wind hooted and laughed at her, and the fog danced beside her and hid her friends. Only the immense black rock in front of her seemed solid and real.

She dug until blisters rose on her fingers and palms. The beach sand seemed to grow heavier with each spadeful of dirt, and she was relieved when Meredith's voice interrupted her digging.

"We've dug down four feet, Nicki, and there's nothing at either the first or second rock."

Nicki glanced up. The sun had warmed the sky behind the rocks and chased the fog away. She could see Meredith, Laura, Christine, and Kim, and they looked as tired as she felt.

"I don't think there's anything in front of rock number three either," she said, pausing to wipe a trickle of perspiration from her forehead. "Jeepers, look at this! I'm freezing *and* sweating!"

"You're just working up internal body heat," Meredith

answered automatically. "I suggest we go on to the next three rocks, but I'll dig alone this time."

"I'm tired," Laura wailed. She held up her hands. "Look at this! Blisters! How am I supposed to go to school next week with my hands looking like this?"

"Your hands will heal," Kim replied firmly, hoisting her shovel onto her shoulder. "Nicki, I'll dig with you on the next rock. Christine and Laura can take the fifth one, and Meredith the sixth."

"We'll be here all day if we keep going like this," Christine grumbled. "And the tide's coming in. Do I need to remind you that we've only got two more days here? Do you really want to spend those two days with blistered hands and aching backs?"

"We want to help Trant," Nicki answered, "and unless you have a better idea, I think we should all get busy before the tide comes up and washes us away."

After Nicki and Kim had displaced three feet of wet sand, Nicki stood up straight and put her hands on her back. "I don't think this is the place, Kim," she said, stretching backward. "Old John Shea didn't bury his treasure here."

"Do you think it's possible that the years have placed tons and tons of sand on top of the treasure?" Kim asked. "Maybe we are in the right place, but we're just not digging deep enough."

"The ocean does bring sand in with the tides, but it takes it out again," Nicki answered. "But I guess anything's possible. Maybe Meredith can ask her professor friend about it." Nicki grabbed her shovel. "Come on, let's go see how the others are doing."

Christine and Laura had dug about two feet down, and when Kim and Nicki arrived, Laura was sitting on a nearby rock examining her hand. "I broke a fingernail,

Nicki Holland," she said, her voice slightly accusing.

"Is that my fault?" Nicki answered, losing patience. "Did you find anything?"

"No, we didn't," Christine answered, her face flushed. She thrust her shovel into the hole in front of her and brushed her hands together. "And I hate this! I've had sand blown into my eyes and hair and I can even feel it between my teeth. I'm ready to quit."

"We have to quit," Nicki answered, pointing down at the ground. Tidewater was seeping into the footprints she had made in the sand. "Tide's coming in. Let's get Meredith and go back. Tonight at low tide we can keep digging."

"I'm wearing gloves," Laura replied firmly. "Strong ones."

"I'm wearing Band-Aids on my hands," Christine answered, raising her shovel to her shoulder, "and a bandanna over my nose. I hate all this sand."

"Hey," Kim said, interrupting the girls, "where's Meredith?" The sun had risen in the sky, changing the color of the beach from gleaming white to the dark gray of wet sidewalk, but there was no sign of Meredith. A pile of sand stood in front of the next rock, but the approaching waves were already doing their best to fill the hole.

"She was there a while ago," Christine said, pointing to the pile of sand. "I saw her."

"How long ago?" Nicki asked, as her heart began to pound with nervous energy. "When did you see her?"

"I dunno," Christine answered, shrugging. "Just before things got real light. I could barely see her digging, but I did see her."

"That's only twenty feet from here," Nicki thought aloud. "How could she just disappear?"

"Maybe she climbed up the rocks and went back to the castle," Laura suggested. "Maybe her shoes were getting wet just like mine are. Come on, Nicki, in a minute we're going to be ankle deep in water."

Nicki ran to the rock where Meredith had been digging. It was one of the larger rocks on the shore, and it jutted out from the rocky cliff like the bow of a boat headed into the sea. The craggy surface of the cliff didn't look like an easy climb, and any footprints Meredith might have left on the beach already had been wiped smooth by the advancing tide. Not even her shovel remained behind.

"Maybe a sea monster took her," Christine suggested, her eyes wide. "A humongous great white shark or a giant sea squid."

"No way," Nicki answered. "Meredith wouldn't go into the water. She was here to dig, and she wouldn't stop digging to go swimming. Besides, the water's cold, and Meredith hates cold water."

"Do you think she was taken by the fairies?" Kim asked quietly. "When night turned to day, the time of half-light, did the fairies take her?"

"That's crazy," Nicki said, turning from the rock to the ocean. The last star had vanished from the sky, and the waves were inching steadily closer and closer to her sneakered feet.

Kim's fingers suddenly gripped Nicki's arm in a strangling grasp. "Look there!" Kim whispered, pointing to the brightening horizon. "Am I seeing things?"

Nicki blinked. Between the water and the sky hovered a shining vision of distant castles, cliffs, and trees. An entire kingdom shimmered on the air over the churning ocean, and it danced in the early morning light.

10

I don't believe it!" Laura whispered. "Silver castles with balconies and forts with towers! Do you all see what I'm seeing?"

Nicki felt her eyes watering. It was too fantastic to be true, but the vision was so real she was sure she would soon see a tiny person come to one of the gleaming windows and wave to her.

"Do you see it, Christine?" Nicki whispered.

"Y-yes," Christine stammered.

"So we all see it," Nicki stated flatly. "We don't know what it is, but we see it plainly."

"It's the fairy fort," Christine said, her eyes never wavering from the startling image. "It's Molly O'Hara's fairy fort."

"It's John Shea's fairy fort," Kim corrected her. "And the treasure is supposed to be inside."

"How do we get there?" Nicki mused. "Take a boat?"

"No," Christine answered. "John Shea didn't have to take a boat. He cooked a leg of mutton or something, and the fairy fort came to him."

"There was something about a cat," Laura whispered. "A cat came out of the fort and—"

"Mrs. Finnegan!" Christine snapped her fingers

and turned away from the mystic city. "Remember Molly's cat? Mrs. Finnegan."

Nicki rolled her eyes. "You can't believe that Mrs. Finnegan guards the fairy fort."

"Why not?" Christine asked. "If we feed the cat a chicken leg or something, maybe she'll go to sleep and the fairy fort will come to us."

"Maybe it came to Meredith," Kim said, glancing at Nicki. "Maybe that's where she went. She found a way into the fairy fort."

"I don't know," Nicki said, turning back to look at the shimmering fairyland. But the mysterious city had disappeared.

"Do any of you see it now?" Nicki asked.

Laura, Kim, and Christine stared out to sea, then shook their heads. "It's gone," Christine said. "It was there, and now it's gone."

Kim looked as though she would cry. "Have we lost Meredith forever?" she said. "What if she's in the fort and we can't get her back?"

Nicki frowned. *Surely such things were totally impossible, but what other explanation could there be?*

"My shoes are wet," Laura interrupted Nicki's thoughts. "We're going to be underwater if we stay here. I think Meredith's safe and sound in the castle. Maybe she had to go in for some reason and just didn't tell us."

"I guess we should go inside," Nicki said, watching the tide advance. She and the others lifted their tools and began to walk back along the beach, but suddenly a distant voice stopped them.

"Hey!" It was Meredith's voice, and Nicki whirled around in relief. "Wait for me!" Meredith called.

The girls waited while Meredith splashed through

the waves. "Whew! I forgot about the tide," Meredith said, breathless. "But you'll never guess what I found. A cave! There's a cave in those rocks!"

"Big deal," Christine said, flipping her damp hair out of her eyes. "We saw the fairy fort."

Meredith's mouth opened in surprise, and Nicki laughed. "It was really weird, and we'll tell you about it inside," Nicki said. "But unless we all want to swim in, we'd better hurry up. Come on, before we get wet again."

The comforting sound of food being scraped from plates greeted them as they entered Molly's kitchen, and she immediately thrust her hands upon her hips and pouted when the girls stomped into the room. "You've given us all a scare, you have," she scolded, thrusting her chin out with every word. "What did you think, that we'd just see you gone and not worry a bit?"

"We're sorry," Nicki said, pulling off her sandy sneakers. "But we just wanted to go out on the beach at low tide."

"I won't ask why," Molly answered, throwing up her hands in hopelessness. "But I want to see you cleaned up and looking like the pretty girls you are instead of a bunch of drowned sea rats. But sure, first you must eat a bit, so take your seats at the table."

"Thanks," Christine said, eagerly pulling out a chair from Molly's massive kitchen table. "I'm starving."

Molly served them a tremendous breakfast of pastries, fruit, cereal, and sausage. "Did you know there's a cave under the western rocks, Molly?" Meredith asked as she buttered her toast. "I saw it today. I went inside, but it was dark and I didn't have a flashlight. I'd like to go back later and explore."

"A cave? Now what would I be doing in a cave?" Molly answered, laughing carefully. Nicki glanced at her sharply. Molly's laughter seemed a bit forced.

"We just heard you grew up here on the island," Nicki said. "So maybe you explored the cave when you were a little kid."

"Nobody goes on the western side of the island," Molly answered firmly. "It's very dangerous. The tide comes in quickly, the rocks are razor sharp in places, and the current is treacherous for swimmers. Several folks have drowned off the western shore in years past, and nobody goes there much. Me own brother was lost off that beach and—" Molly gulped and shook her head. "I don't even like to think about it."

"We're sorry," Meredith said quietly. "Maybe no one knows about the cave because it's covered by water when the tide is in. But it looked really interesting, and I want to explore it when the tide's out again."

"Do you think the treasure's in there?" Christine mumbled, her mouth full of banana-nut muffin.

Meredith raised an eyebrow. "Could be. We won't know until we look, but we need to bring a flashlight when we go out again."

"I'll do anything but dig," Laura said, looking again at her hands. "Three blisters and one broken nail is too high a price to pay."

"Which brings me to one other question," Nicki said, folding her hands on the table. She watched Molly's face carefully as she asked, "Have you ever seen a city on the water? A shiny city with castles and towers and gleaming trees? A city that just floats between the water and the sky?"

Molly's eyes darted rapidly to the western window, and she seemed to physically shrink as she turned fearfully away from the window. "A shiny city?" she finally asked, her voice cracking. "What kind of idiot would go around looking for floating cities? I'd be locked up in an asylum if I saw that, wouldn't I now?"

"But you told us you've seen a fairy fort," Christine pointed out. "You said you've seen it from the kitchen window."

Meredith kicked Nicki under the table. "Did *you* see a shiny city?" Meredith whispered to Nicki, her dark eyes wide. "This morning?"

Nicki nodded silently to Meredith, who nearly choked on the bite of toast she was chewing. She didn't have a chance to explain, though, because at that moment the kitchen door swung open and in walked Mr. Shea, leading the way for his son, who hobbled in on crutches with his leg in a heavy plaster cast.

Trant was home, and Kim's face lit up like a kid's under a Christmas tree.

11

"W elcome home, me boy." Molly O'Hara left the bowl of batter she was stirring and gripped Trant's face with her floury hands to give him a loud, smacky kiss. "It's good to have you back where you belong."

"It's good to be back," Trant answered, his eyes immediately wandering to where Kim sat at the kitchen table. Trant blushed slightly as he added, "I didn't want to miss anything."

The sound of heavy boots scraping the mat at the door made Nicki turn. Maurice O'Griffin stood there, his hat in his hand. "Glad to see the boy's better, John," he said to Mr. Shea. "Last night he didn't look very pert, did he now?"

"Not a bit," Mr. Shea agreed, smiling in relief. "But the doctor says he'll be fine if he takes it easy."

"Coffee, Maurice?" Molly offered, hurrying away to the coffee pot. "John, I know you'll want a cup."

Maurice slid into an empty chair and propped his feet up on a small footstool by the kitchen fireplace. "Aye, I'll just make meself at home, Molly. I have to wait on the other bloke I brought over—he wants to poke around the beach a bit. I've known some Englishmen who were a bit daft, but this one's plain swarmy in the head, if you're asking me."

Meredith's head rose in a jerk. "An Englishman?

Are you talking about Professor Jeremy Fulton?"

Maurice took the steaming cup of coffee Molly offered him and nodded at Meredith. "Aye, I believe that is the chap's name. Anyway, he asked John here if he minded a visit to Cravenhill Island, and we brought him over with us."

Meredith's face shone. "Professor Fulton is researching on your island," she announced to Mr. Shea. "How honored you must feel!"

Mr. Shea shrugged. "I'd feel more honored if he had in mind to buy the place. We've been running that advert in the paper for months now, and no one's even bothered to come out here."

"I've been taking the advert to the papers for you, just like you said," Maurice said, nodding to Mr. Shea. "'Tis a shame you can't sell. When do you have to have the tax money in?"

"By the end of the month," Mr. Shea said in a flat, expressionless voice. "Then it's all over for us. Cravenhill Castle will go on the auction block, and the Sheas will be off to Dingle to rent a duplex."

He forced a smile and ruffled Trant's hair. "But nothing for you to worry about, me boy. I rather fancy you'll like living in Dingle. There you'll find more people, more fun, and the prettiest girls you've ever seen!"

"I can see plenty of pretty girls right here," Trant answered, looking at Kim.

Laura giggled, and Nicki kicked her under the table. Meredith ignored the commotion and timidly tapped Mr. Shea on the arm. "Maybe it's not all over for you," she said. "Professor Fulton is just the man we need to see to help find the treasure. Maybe we'll even find something today."

Mr. Shea lifted his bushy brows, and Maurice

O'Griffin slapped his leg in merriment. "Ah, sure, and the famous Shea treasure is calling out to be brought up today," Maurice said, whooping in delight. "And you girls are going to save everything."

"It's that typical American can-do attitude," Mr. Shea said, shaking his head. "Americans are funny that way. They think that with a little luck and perseverance, they can do anything."

"Well, it works for us," Nicki answered, lifting her chin proudly. "And we're not going to do it alone. Trant is going to help us, if he can."

"Not today he's not," Molly said, bringing her hand firmly down upon the oak table. "He's staying on the sofa where I can watch him, and he's going to rest that leg. Maybe tomorrow, Trant, you can be up and about, but not today. Sorry, girls, but you're on your own."

"That's okay," Meredith said, standing up. "We'll show you what American ingenuity can do."

"You're going to be sorry you bragged about Americans," Laura pouted as they walked down the garden path on their way to the beach. "What if we don't find anything? We'll be embarrassed."

"We'll find something," Meredith answered. "Now that Professor Fulton is here, maybe we can get some answers about the beach and the cave and the rocks. It would help, you see, if we knew what the beach looked like five hundred years ago, when John Shea first saw the treasure."

"*Supposedly* saw the treasure, you mean," Laura said. "We still haven't seen anything to prove that the entire story isn't a crazy legend."

"It can't be just a legend," Nicki said, shaking her head. "We've seen too many weird things on this island. You know, being here—" she waved her hands at the beautiful greenery around them, "—being here has opened my eyes to all kinds of new things. We've seen flying fire balls, fairy cities on the ocean—"

"And don't forget the cat," Meredith interrupted. "I forgot to tell you, but Mrs. Finnegan actually led me to the cave. I was on the beach, digging away, when Mrs. Finnegan came up and brushed against my legs. I reached down to pet her, but she darted away and starting running up into the rocks. I watched her for a minute, then she disappeared, almost before my eyes."

"Spooky," Laura said, shivering. "I would have run away."

"That's because you're not a scientist," Meredith answered. "*I* went up to investigate, and found the opening of a small cave. You can't see the opening from the beach because a rock nearly covers it, but once you stoop to get inside, it's a pretty big cave. I couldn't tell how big, though, because it was pitch black inside and I didn't have a flashlight. But my voice echoed when I called out, and it smelled wet, so the cave is probably filled with water when the tide's in."

"We'll get my flashlight," Nicki promised, "and we'll go back when the tide goes out again." She pulled playfully on a low-hanging tree branch, and the branch bobbed, raining dew upon their heads. Laura and Christine squealed as the shower fell upon them.

"The tide goes out again tonight," Meredith said, grinning at Nicki. "I can't wait. But now we really need to find Professor Fulton. Just think, we were going to Dingle to talk to him, and he came to us!"

They found Professor Jeremy Fulton several yards down the rocky western shore. Perched on a narrow outcropping of rock, he was above the now-submerged beach the girls had explored that morning, and below the plateau where they now walked. They heard the professor before they actually saw him—he was talking to himself and the moist wind carried his words to their ears.

"Typical sedimentary," Nicki heard him say. "Black in color. No evidence of metamorphic samples."

"Hello, Professor Fulton!" Meredith called, galloping over to the rocky edge. She hopped up on a large black rock and grinned down at him. "Remember me? From the train?"

Nicki and the others hurried over in time to see him climb up and shake Meredith's hand energetically. "Meredith," he said, the wind blowing his wispy hair. "It's nice to see you again. I had no idea I'd find you on Cravenhill Island."

Nicki thought Professor Fulton looked completely different now than he had in his tweed coat. In khaki shorts, short-sleeved black T-shirt (with "introvert" in tiny letters across the chest), and heavy climbing boots, he looked less like a professor and more like an explorer. At his waist he wore a thick leather belt from which dangled a coiled rope, a small pick axe, a tape recorder, several empty plastic containers, and a bottle of Gatorade. His best feature was his eyes, which were direct and friendly.

"Professor, these are my friends," Meredith said, motioning toward the girls. "Nicki, Kim, Christine, and Laura. We've been working out here today, too."

"Really?" the professor asked, settling back on a rock and folding his arms. "I should think you girls had better things to do than crawl around on rocks."

"Most people would think so," Christine spoke up, flipping her hair back from her face. "But no-o-o. My friends' idea of a vacation is a crazy treasure hunt."

"Treasure?" Professor Fulton cocked his head and gave Meredith a lopsided grin. "Seriously?"

"Yes," Meredith said, refusing to be embarrassed. "And we wanted to ask you something about it. Suppose a man buried a treasure here beneath these rocks about five hundred years ago. What are the odds of it being found today?"

Professor Fulton whistled in surprise and took a sip from his bottle of Gatorade before answering. "It's hard to answer a geomorphological question like that without five hundred years of weather reports," he said. "But beaches are not forever, you know. Tectonic motion changes the location of the ocean basins, and what is shoreline today may be underwater or far inland tomorrow. In addition to these long-term processes, there are natural forces that work to change beaches."

"Are you understanding any of this?" Laura whispered to Nicki. "I'm not."

"As long as Meredith is, we're okay," Nicki whispered back.

"The littoral conveyor belt moves sand along beaches," the professor continued. "When waves come into a beach, they normally approach it at an angle. After having washed up on the beach, however, they flow straight back into the water under the influence of gravity. Thus, the net motion of water and sand is a sawtooth pattern in and out. Over periods of days or weeks, individual grains of sand along a beach will be moved slowly up and down the beach."

"I see," Meredith said. "Anything else?"

The professor shrugged. "Storms play a great role in shaping a beach," he added. "Stormy weather produces bigger waves than usual, and the bigger the waves, the more sand is moved."

"So this beach is nothing like it was five hundred years ago?" Nicki asked, feeling disappointed.

The professor smiled indulgently. "These aren't the actual grains of sand, no. But the sand that is moved out and away during a storm is usually returned by calmer weather. Or, in the case of this island, the sand that is eroded on this rocky coast is probably dumped on the eastern side of the island."

"So these rocks," Meredith said, waving her hand to indicate the huge black slabs that lined the beach, "were probably more in the center of the island five hundred years ago."

The professor nodded. "That's a sound assumption," he said. Meredith looked at Nicki. "Then we could dig until our palms bleed," she said. "If John Shea the First buried his treasure in the sand, it's probably a mile out to sea by now."

"But maybe it's in the cave," Kim said, her eyes shining. "He could have put it in the cave, couldn't he?"

Professor Fulton regarded Kim carefully. "Cave?" he asked with interest. "You found a cave? Where?"

"Never mind the cave," Nicki said, leaning on a rock near the professor. "Do you mind if I ask a question?"

"Shoot," Professor Fulton answered.

"It may sound silly," Nicki said, looking down at her feet. "But do you believe in fairies?"

The professor tossed back his head and laughed—for too long, Nicki thought. "No, I don't believe in fairies," he said finally, rubbing his stomach as if it ached from laughing too hard. "I believe everything on earth has a scientific explanation." He raised a silver eyebrow. "What do you believe?"

"Never mind," Nicki answered, standing up. She pulled Meredith's arm. "Come on, Meredith, we need to go check on Trant. It was nice to see you, Professor. Happy digging."

Meredith frowned as Nicki led her away, and once they were out of hearing range, Meredith stopped in her tracks and put her hands on her hips. "I'm not going another step unless you tell me why you jerked me away from the professor like that," she demanded.

"I just had a feeling," Nicki explained, opening her hands wide. "It just seems too coincidental that Professor Fulton has shown up here on the island and is looking around where we were this morning. What if *he's* looking for the treasure? What if he talked to Trant or to Maurice—"

"Probably everyone in Dingle knows the legend," Kim pointed out. "So maybe the professor was here to look for treasure himself."

"Yeah, that makes sense," Laura said, twirling her blonde hair around her finger. "You said he was here to study weather, right? Why couldn't he study that in Dingle? Why would he have to come out to Cravenhill Island?"

"You're talking about a future Nobel prize winner!" Meredith stormed, her eyebrows knitted together in a frown. "And he's my friend!"

"I'm sorry, Meredith," Nicki said smoothly. "We're not accusing him of anything. But if he finds the treasure, he'll claim it for science, won't he? Do you think the treasure will do Trant's family any good if it has to sit in some museum somewhere?"

"I hadn't thought of that," Meredith replied, crossing her arms. "All right. But you'll never convince me the professor's a bad guy. He's really above reproach."

"Okay, I believe you," Nicki answered. "But right now I'm not sure what's going on. Molly's blaming all the weird things on fairies, and your professor says everything that happens has a scientific explanation. I don't know what to believe."

They spent the afternoon in the huge drawing room, enjoying the castle's relaxed atmosphere. Trant, his leg propped up on the sofa with pillows, chattered and played Monopoly with Kim, Christine, and Laura while Meredith read a book from Mrs. Shea's library. Mrs. Shea and Mrs. Cushman sat in a corner talking, and Molly O'Hara bustled through the room with trays of freshly baked biscuits and cups of steaming tea. Nicki lay on the thick carpet in front of the fireplace, her head propped up on an overstuffed pillow. She didn't want to play games or talk. She wanted to think, but her mind spun around and around in circles, going nowhere.

Finally she leaned her head on her elbow and looked up at the two women. "Does this castle have any interesting stories?" she asked Mrs. Shea. "Ghost stories? Births, deaths, that kind of thing?"

"Nicki, how gruesome," Mrs. Cushman chided, but Mrs. Shea only smiled.

"Actually, yes," Mrs. Shea replied, delicately

punching her needle through the cloth in her embroidery hoop. "In 1690, the battle of two English kings nearly killed off the Sheas. That John Shea of Cravenhill gathered his sons and his brothers around the table in the dining room. There were ten men all together, and they ate breakfast, kissed their wives and children, and went off to join King James and his troops on the southern bank of the Boyne River. None of them ever returned to Cravenhill."

"They were all killed?" Nicki whispered.

Mrs. Shea nodded soberly. "Aye. But the fourth John Shea's wife, Dervorgilla, was pregnant with yet another child, who was born to be the fifth John Shea."

"How terrible that must have been for her!" Nicki said, imagining how it would feel to lose your husband, sons, and other relatives in one day.

"Aye, the family was nearly brought completely to loss, for the men had invested their fortunes in the cause," Mrs. Shea went on. "But Dervorgilla sold something—I'm not quite sure what it was—and the family had enough money to survive for some time. She quite literally saved the family from starvation."

"What did she sell?" Nicki wondered aloud. "Maybe she found the lost Shea treasure!"

"I doubt that," Mrs. Shea laughed, "for though she saved the family, she didn't make the family rich. But she is quite the Shea heroine. Her portrait hangs in the great hall yonder, have you seen it?"

"I didn't really notice it," Nicki confessed. "I saw a bunch of old pictures."

"They're real people, Nicki dear," Mrs. Shea said softly. "Our people, who fought and died for Ireland, who worked this land and built this castle." Mrs. Shea's chin quivered slightly. "And to think that death and destruction and famine couldn't kill off the Sheas, but the simple matter of taxes will do us in—" Mrs. Shea stopped and made an effort to steady her voice. "The unlucky thirteenth John Shea and his luckless wife will be the last Sheas to live here."

Mrs. Cushman patted Mrs. Shea's hand comfortingly, and Nicki stood up and went into the great hall. There were many pictures of proud and stern-looking people, but finally she found the picture with only one word under it, "Dervorgilla." The lady in the painting was lovely, with faint blue eyes, an oval face, and dark hair pulled neatly back with a ribbon. But the lady's pride outshone her beauty. Dervorgilla looked as though she had battled the worst circumstances in life, and won.

Strangely enough, the portrait of Dervorgilla looked straight into the dining room, at the very table where the fourth John Shea ate breakfast before leaving to die in the Battle of the Boyne. Nicki felt a sudden chill. Mrs. Shea hadn't said anything about ghosts, but Nicki felt as though the eyes of every Shea ancestor looked down at her, mutely asking what she would do to find their long-lost treasure.

13

A t six o'clock, after one of Molly's famous dinners, Nicki
and her friends said goodbye to Trant and scooted
quickly out the kitchen door. Kim walked slowly, and
Nicki knew she hadn't wanted to leave Trant's side.

"You don't have to come with us," Nicki told Kim
as they walked. "I know you don't have a lot of time to
spend with Trant, and if you'd rather stay inside, it's
okay."

"No," Kim replied firmly, glancing up at Nicki.
"Though I want to be with him, I think this is the best way
I can help him. Besides, he's tired and his pain medication
has made him sleepy. I will let him sleep, and help you
find the treasure for his family."

Nicki patted the flashlight in her jacket pocket.
"This time," she told Kim, "I'm sure we'll find *something*,
even if it's only a cave. Even that will be interesting."

"Are you sure the tide's out?" Laura asked nervously as they made their way down the garden path to the
beach. "I'm not getting my shoes all wet again."

"The tide will be out," Meredith promised. "Your
dainty little feet will stay nice and dry."

Christine giggled, Laura pouted, and Nicki rolled
her eyes. Laura was entirely too prissy sometimes, but
they had come to accept her as she was. She always came
through in a pinch.

Nicki pointed through the greenery to James Murray's toolshed. "Do you think we'll need anything?" she asked. "What if the treasure is *buried* in the cave? Or what if barnacles have it stuck to the rocks?"

"It's probably a good idea to take a shovel and one of those pick axes," Meredith said, striding forward and opening the door to the toolshed. "Christine, grab that rope there, too, okay? You never know what we'll need."

Kim shouldered a shovel, Christine grabbed the rope, and Laura gingerly held the pick axe between her fingers as if it were a dead rat. "For heaven's sake, let me carry it," Meredith snapped, snatching the long pole away from Laura. "It's not going to bite you."

"It's dirty," Laura said, making a face. "I'm wearing rayon, for heaven's sake, and rayon has to be dry-cleaned."

Nicki shook her head and stepped outside by the door to close it when the last girl had come out. She felt aggressive and eager, really on her toes, and she nearly jumped out of her skin when a hand touched her shoulder.

"What are you girls up to now, if you dinna mind me asking?"

Nicki turned and saw James Murray, his dark brows knitted together in concern. "We, uh, we're going to do some digging on the beach," she said, smiling politely. "Don't worry, we'd never dig in your garden."

"You're not going to look for treasure again, are you?" James asked, clucking his tongue like a scolding teacher. "It's bad luck, I tell you, to seek what the fairies have guarded for years. Remember my burnt tree? It was a warning from the fairies. Remember Trant's unfortunate accident? Another warning. You girls are going to call the curse of Cravenhill upon yourselves next if you aren't careful."

"I thought you didn't believe in fairies or the treasure," Nicki said.

"One has to wonder about such things," James replied. "And I've seen enough lately to make me wonder if we might be tempting a fairy's curse."

"It would seem to me that the curse of Cravenhill, if there is such a thing, has been activated already," Meredith pointed out. "Maybe finding treasure would change things for the better around here. Trant's fall was an accident. That ball of light—well, I don't know what it was, but I don't believe in fairies. And if we *don't* find the treasure, the Sheas will lose Cravenhill all together."

Meredith tilted her head and regarded James Murray with open curiosity. "By the way, Mr. Murray, what would you do if the Sheas had to put the castle on the auction block?"

James Murray smiled. "Why, nothing," he answered. "No matter who owns the castle, I'm the Cravenhill grounds keeper. Ah, sure, I'd miss the Sheas, wonderful people that they are, but I'd miss me home more, so I'll not leave it."

Nicki raised an eyebrow in Meredith's direction. "Thank you, Mr. Murray, for the warning," Nicki said. "But we'll be back in just a little while."

"Storm's coming up," James Murray muttered, raising his finger into the wind. "Be careful!"

They had been on the sandy beach for no more than three minutes when Nicki realized James Murray was right. The breeze, which had been light and soothing, suddenly grew hard and pushy, as if a monster gale had come sliding down over the island. A swollen cloud moved overhead to block the sun, and the wind grew cold—a breeze that knifed lungs and made the girls' skin tingle. "Jeepers, this is terrible," Christine yelled, struggling to be heard above the moaning of the wind. "It's like Mother Nature is trying to stop us from going on!"

Nicki didn't believe Christine was right, but as they pressed into the wind and moved steadily up the beach toward the rocky shore, Nicki felt an unknown dread clutch her heart. Something was wrong, something undefinable. The air felt unnatural, the water looked as if it had been altered somehow, and even the castle on top of the hill looked more like a cardboard silhouette than a real place where friends and a warm fire waited inside.

"Meredith!" she yelled above the wind. "Something feels weird. Do you feel it, too?"

"Yes." Meredith froze in her steps and nodded mutely at the beach ahead. A few feet in front of them, gray arms of rain reached down from the clouds and began to soak the rocky cliff and the sand.

"It's going to be a big storm," Meredith told Nicki. "What do we do? Run back to the castle or try to make it to the cave?"

Nicki looked around. The castle lay at least fifteen minutes away, plus they'd have to run through the gardens while trees moaned and thrashed around them. She shuddered at the thought of meeting another ball of lightning in the storm. Ahead, only a few feet away, the unknown cave waited, and rain couldn't hurt them in a cave, could it?

"Let's run for the cave," Nicki yelled, motioning for the other girls to follow her. They began to jog breathlessly through the rain and wailing wind, and Meredith led them past the first few outcropping rocks. She paused in front of one rock, and Nicki had to squint to see through the rain that stung her flesh like tiny needles. Only a few feet away, sea waves rose up and snarled at them.

Meredith motioned for the others to wait while she climbed up a boulder and searched among the rocks for the cave's opening. "Hurry, Meredith," Laura wailed, hugging herself in misery. Like Nicki, Laura was drenched. Nicki, Kim, Laura, and Christine huddled together, their backs to the fierce sea, while Meredith poked and prodded the rocks. Suddenly Nicki heard the smack of objects falling around her, and her heart began to pound as something hit her on the head.

Laura screamed, Christine flailed her arms hysterically, and Kim sank back against the rocks, her face deathly pale. Something slapped Nicki in the face and fell at her feet, and she instinctively leaped back. Inches away from her shoes, a small fish flopped in the sand. Other fish were falling fiercely from the sky with such force that they actually bounced when they hit the earth.

"This is too weird," Christine screamed, pulling on Nicki's arm with both hands. "Come on, let's get out of here."

"We can't," Nicki yelled back, struggling to break Christine's grip. "Meredith's still up there in the rocks! Besides, we're too far from the castle."

"James warned us," Laura hollered, as a long, black eel dropped from the sky and coiled around her neck. Laura went as pale as paper and sank to her knees in the sand. Nicki yanked the eel off with a jerk and flung it away.

"Don't faint," Nicki warned her sternly, wiping her hand on her jeans, "or we'll leave you here."

Just then Meredith tapped Nicki on the shoulder. "I found it," she cried, ducking as a disgusting jellied sea creature nearly hit her in the face. "Come on, and we'll be out of this mess."

The girls grabbed the tools they had brought and followed Meredith in a single line up and over the rocks. As sea creatures continued to fall from the skies around them, they found the entrance to the cave and gratefully stepped inside.

14

The cave yawned before them in blackness. There was no sound but Laura's frightened hiccuping and Christine's rattled breathing. "Nicki?" Meredith asked, her voice echoing in the formless cavern. "This is a good time to get out your flashlight."

Nicki pulled her small flashlight from her pocket and turned it on. "Is everybody okay?" she asked, shining the light on the faces of her friends. "Did anybody get hurt by all that falling stuff?"

"That was too awful to even think about," Christine said, shuddering. She pulled a damp tissue from her pocket and loudly blew her nose. "You can't tell me now, Nicki, that something weird isn't going on around here—something *supernatural*, I mean. Eels and fish and sea toads don't just drop from the sky and hit people."

"It was almost as though the fairies knew what we were up to and decided to throw things at us," Laura said, wrapping her wet jacket closer around her. "I'm ready to quit. I want to go home."

"We'll go back to the castle soon," Nicki promised.

"Not to the castle, I want to go *home*," Laura retorted, stamping her foot. "I'm tired of this crazy stuff. Ireland can keep its fairies and treasure and shamrocks and everything else. I'm ready to go home to Florida."

"What about Trant?" Kim asked softly. The head of the shovel gave off a metallic echo as Kim lowered it to the ground. "I'm ready to look for treasure, Nicki. Let's do what we have to do, and then get out of here."

"Okay," Nicki said, shining the light in front of them. The tiny beam of the pocket flashlight did little to light up the room of stone they found themselves in, and only by bouncing the beam off the walls could Nicki determine how large a cave they had found. The walls were black like the rocks around them, but it was obvious that tidewaters had been flowing there regularly, for the walls were smooth.

"It looks like silky chocolate pudding," Meredith said, rubbing her hand over the cavern wall. "With little sparkles inside it."

"That's crazy," Christine said, stepping boldly forward into the darkness.

"Don't step anywhere without the light," Meredith warned her. "We don't know where the floor might just drop off. The water comes in here during the day, remember, and—" She paused.

"What?" Nicki asked.

"There might be something in here with us," Meredith finished.

"Like what?" Laura asked, still hiccuping.

Meredith shrugged. "Like a fish or something, I don't know. Let's take it step by step and see what we can find."

"Do you think any of the John Sheas of Cravenhill ever found this cave?" Kim asked as they cautiously stepped forward into the beam of Nicki's flashlight.

"That's probably a sound assumption," Meredith answered, gazing upward at the cave ceiling a few inches above their heads. "But I asked Trant, and he doesn't know anything about it. I guess he just never has gotten around to exploring this far."

"Well, we hope at least one John Shea knew about this cave," Nicki remarked, shining the light in a clockwise pattern as they walked forward in a shoulder-to-shoulder line. "We hope the first John Shea left his treasure here."

"No fairies yet," Kim remarked lightly as they carefully stepped forward. "And Laura, would you please not grip my arm so tightly? You're cutting off my circulation."

"Sorry," Laura muttered.

"It's so dark in here," Christine whispered. "So dark and so forever. Do you think it has an end?"

"Every cave has an end," Meredith answered calmly, not even flinching when her foot splashed into a puddle unexpectedly. "We just might not be able to find it."

"We are staying close to a wall, aren't we?" Christine asked. "I don't want to get lost in here and never come out."

"We won't get lost," Nicki answered. "Listen, and you can hear the sea and the storm outside. All we have to do is walk toward the sound." A misty doubt darted through Nicki's mind, but she dismissed it. Of course they could find their way out.

"What's that ahead?" Christine squealed, her high voice ping-ponging off the cave walls. "All shiny and black and—"

"It's just a big puddle," Nicki answered, shining the light ahead of them. They walked closer and found a large puddle of sea water that stretched from the right cave wall to the left. "It's only about five feet across, so we can jump it or wade through it."

"I'm jumping," Christine said, backing up for a running start. "Me, too," Kim answered, gripping her shovel firmly.

"I can't jump that far," Laura wailed, squeezing her hands into fists as Christine and Kim jumped with no problem.

"Laura, you can wade through if you want to," Meredith said, grinning. Meredith sized up the puddle, stepped back, grasped her pick axe firmly, and sprinted forward, clearing the puddle easily.

Christine, Kim, and Meredith stood on the other side and looked at Nicki. Nicki turned the light on Laura. "If you're going to wade, do it now," Nicki said. "I'll keep the light on you as you go across, but I'm ready to jump."

Laura scrunched up her face in dismay as she pulled off her damp tennis shoes and socks. Gingerly holding them in her fingers, she stuck the toes of one foot into the water. "What if it's deep?" she whimpered. "What if I drop out of sight?"

"It's probably only two or three inches deep," Meredith said, nodding confidently. "Scientifically, it couldn't be deep unless a crosscurrent existed to wear away the rock, and there is no crosscurrent. Trust me, Laura, you'll be okay."

Laura crinkled her nose in protest, but put both feet into the water and began inching her way through the puddle. "If you walk faster you'll be across," Christine called out impatiently. "Come on, we don't have all day."

"Speaking of all day, what time is it?" Meredith asked. "I can't see my watch."

"Just a minute, and I'll check," Nicki said, moving the flashlight from Laura's feet to the watch on her wrist. "It's six-forty—"

"Aaaaaeeeeee!" Laura screamed, splashing wildly in the water. "Something's got me!"

Nicki jerked the flashlight back in Laura's direction. Screaming in honest fear, Laura scrambled out of the pool with a large, orange-red creature clinging stubbornly to her big toe.

"A crab!" Meredith announced proudly. "I told you there might be sea creatures in here!"

"Get it off!" Laura screamed, her eyes blazing in the faint light. "Help me!"

Meredith raised the pick axe and brought it down firmly on the crab's pinching claw. The animal released Laura's toe and backed away from the girls, its protruding eyes watching them warily.

"Guess what?" Nicki said, backing up. She laughed. "I'm not wading, I'm jumping!" She ran and cleared the crab and the puddle of sea water easily, then held the flashlight on Laura's offended toe. There was no bleeding, only a bright pink spot where the crab had staked its claim.

"I hate this!" Laura stormed, tears running down her cheeks. "I really hate this!"

"Don't worry, just put on your shoes and socks and keep them on," Meredith told her. "We'll be done soon."

When Laura was ready to move on, the girls continued their journey through the cavern. "Look how the walls glisten in the light," Nicki said, letting the beam from her flashlight playfully bounce along the walls. "They look like they've been dusted in pixie dust."

"Just don't say fairy dust," Christine warned, "or I'm outta here."

"Seriously, isn't there a name for that kind of rock?" Nicki asked, tugging on Meredith's sleeve.

"Well, Professor Fulton would know all about that," Meredith replied smoothly. "But you didn't want to tell him about the cave, so I guess we'll never know, will we?"

Nicki rolled her eyes. "Okay, maybe I was wrong about the professor. Maybe it's James Murray who's after the treasure. You noticed that he really doesn't care who buys the castle. He's staying here no matter what."

"He grew up here, too, didn't he?" Kim asked. "Maybe he found this cave when he was young, and he's waiting for the Sheas to leave before he can claim it. Maybe that's why he warned us about all that fairy stuff."

"Maybe Molly O'Hara knows where the treasure is and isn't saying," Laura added. She sniffed. "And all her attention to poor precious Trant is just an act. I'll bet she's counting the days until they leave, then she can pull out the treasure and buy the castle herself."

"I don't know about that," Nicki said. "She seems pretty genuine to me."

"Well, I refuse to believe in fairies," Meredith said, "and I don't believe in bad luck, either. So if the treasure is on this island, someone can find it. Maybe not us, but someone can."

"Stop," Nicki said, shining the light steadily ahead of them. The passageway through which they had been walking narrowed and ascended gradually, forming a small tunnel. At the end of the tunnel Nicki could see one small opening. "We can only get through that passageway one at a time," she said, stepping closer. "And we're going to have to stoop down to do it."

"I'm scared," Laura whimpered, clutching Kim's arm. "Let's just forget it and go back, okay?"

"We've come this far, we might as well go on," Meredith said, stooping behind Nicki. "If you were going to hide a treasure, would you put it right out there in the open? I wouldn't. I'd put it back here, out of the way, where no one else could find it."

"But we don't know what's in there!" Laura wailed, genuinely scared. "You've heard of the Loch Ness Monster, right? What if its cousin is sleeping in there?"

"With all that screaming, you're going to wake it up," Christine said, glaring at Laura. "And it won't be happy. So hush up and just follow us. The sooner we find the end of this cave, the sooner we'll be out of here."

"Hey, you know what this reminds me of?" Kim said, gently snapping her fingers. "Remember Molly's story about the fairy fort? John Shea went into the first room and found the bowl and razor. He went into the *second* room and saw the treasure."

"So if the story is a code for where the treasure really is—" Meredith interrupted, her eyes shining.

"—then this is the entrance to the second room!" Kim finished, nodding confidently.

"You've forgotten one thing," Christine pointed out. "In the story, the old man gave John Shea a warning. He said if John touched anything in the room, he'd never come out alive."

"All treasure tales have warnings," Meredith said, shaking her head. "It's part of the routine. It doesn't mean anything."

"Wow!" Nicki breathed, staring at the narrow opening ahead of them. "I guess this is it, then. Is everybody ready?"

Christine looked at Nicki. "What are we waiting for?" she asked, pushing her damp hair from her eyes. "Let's go on. Whether we find the treasure or meet a monster, I'm ready."

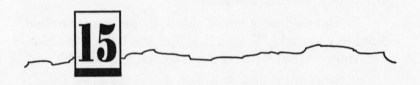

15

Nicki felt Meredith's hand on her back as she stooped to enter the passageway. She crawled forward about three feet, then the rock above her head rose and she found herself in another cavern. Her sneakers crunched on the rocky sand beneath her feet as she inched her way in, and her flashlight revealed nothing of the cavern but an enveloping blackness. Shivering, she turned the flashlight behind her until Meredith, Kim, Christine, and Laura were safely in.

"We're all here," Meredith said, standing upright. "But where are we?"

"I don't know," Nicki answered, shining the flashlight around. The beam of light only reached about six feet in front of them, revealing a sandy floor and darkness. "This place must be *huge*," Nicki breathed, her whisper slipping away in a ghostly echo. "It's like the inside of Cravenhill Island is one big cave."

"We could be right under the castle," Meredith said, her eyes shining in the dim light. "Imagine that! If we could somehow climb up, we could cut through the rock and pop up at Molly's kitchen table."

"I wish I were there now," Laura grumbled, her teeth chattering, "instead of here."

"Well, how do we explore this place?" Nicki asked. "It's so big."

Meredith shrugged. "Let's follow this wall of stone here by the opening. Hopefully, we'll come around in a circle. If not, we can always come back until we find this opening again."

"That sounds good," Nicki said. She shined the light on the solid gray-brown wall of stone, then the girls began moving forward through the cavern. "It's cold in here," Laura complained, "and my clothes are wet. I'll catch pneumonia, for sure."

"No, you won't," Nicki answered. "We'll all be just fine."

"What are these things under my feet?" Christine grumbled. "I keep tripping over some kind of big rock."

"Me, too," Kim added.

Nicki stopped so abruptly that Meredith ran into her. "I don't know what those are, but I feel them, too," Nicki said, lowering the light to the sand at their feet. The floor of the cavern was littered with dark red stones. "What are these?" Nicki said, stooping to pick up one of the rocks. She held it on her palm and turned it over in the light. "Look at this, you guys, it's in the perfect shape of an *x*."

"Or a cross," Kim added, gazing over Meredith's shoulder.

"It looks like someone carved it," Christine said. "Jeepers, do you think this is some ancient burial ground or something? We should get out of here!"

"No, it's just a rock," Meredith said, shrugging. "One unusual rock does not a burial ground make, Christine. Calm that imagination of yours!"

"But there's more than one!" Christine said, pointing to the other cross-shaped stones on the ground. "Lots more!"

"Forget it, Chris," Meredith snapped. "I'm not going to be spooked out of this place, especially not when we're so close to solving everything."

Nicki laughed and slipped the unusual rock into her pocket. As they began moving again, the beam of her flashlight hit something that glimmered through the darkness.

"What's that?" Laura gasped. "It looked like something shiny!"

Nicki positioned the flashlight upon the mysterious object. "It's a chest!" Meredith exclaimed, rushing forward. "Just like the ones in our room at the castle!"

The girls examined the large wooden chest with rusty brass hinges and clasps. "It's the treasure chest!" Laura squealed, her fears apparently forgotten. She and Christine danced a little jig while Laura sang, "I can't believe we found the treasure!"

"It's just a chest," Meredith said, kneeling on the hard surface. She and Kim tugged at the lid with no success. "The locks and latches have rusted shut. Either we pry the lid off, or we carry the chest out of here."

"There's no way we can carry it," Nicki said, trying to move the heavy chest. "It weighs a ton."

"There's always the pick axe," Christine said, pointing to the tool Meredith had laid in the sand. "I say we open it and carry the gold out in our pockets."

"But old chests are valuable," Nicki pointed out. "My mom bought one at an antique shop once and it wasn't cheap. We shouldn't destroy the chest."

"Then we'll open it carefully," Meredith said, picking up the pick axe. "Move back everybody, in case something breaks off. I wouldn't want to hit anyone in the eye."

The other girls stood back while Meredith skillfully aimed the pointed end of the axe head toward the first rusted latch on the chest. Nicki held the light steadily on the latch. "Careful, Meredith," she warned.

Meredith swung the axe handle with remarkable accuracy, and the latch cracked. "Yea!" Kim cheered, the sound of her applause echoing in the vast chamber. "Now do the other one!"

Meredith aimed the axe head again, swung, and the other latch burst. The girls eagerly clambered around the chest while Nicki came closer and held the light over their heads. "Okay," Nicki breathed, glancing down at Meredith. "Let's open it and see what we've found."

The lid of the chest was heavy. Christine, Laura, Kim, and Meredith tugged and pulled and lifted for three or four minutes before the lid actually budged. The chest cracked, the metal protested, then the girls swung the lid up and back.

Nicki shone the light inside the chest. Inside lay the barely recognizable remains of a small person, and Nicki was afraid for a moment that Christine was right, that they had stumbled onto a burial ground. "Is that a baby?" Nicki gasped, looking at the moldy wet remains of a baby's dress.

"No, it's a doll," Meredith said, tenderly lifting out a porcelain doll. Its clothes were a mess, but the doll's delicate porcelain face and limbs were in perfect condition.

"How disappointing," Christine cried, scanning the rest of the trunk's contents. "There's no treasure here! This is only a bunch of junk! It looks like old toys and books and what used to be clothes, I think."

Nicki gave her flashlight to Laura and knelt beside the trunk. "This isn't junk," she said, lifting out a moldy book. The book was ruined and dark with age, but a brass nameplate on the cover was still legible in the dim light. "Dervorgilla Shea," Nicki read, breathing quietly in the darkness. "I know who this belongs to. Dervorgilla Shea is the lady who lost her husband and sons in the Battle of the Boyne."

"So how did this junk get down here?" Laura asked, shining the flashlight beam once again on the doll. "*Why* did she put this stuff down here?"

"I don't know," Nicki answered, shaking her head. "Unless it was her way of burying her past and getting on with her new life. I'll bet these journals explained everything she went through, but they're too badly damaged to read."

"Maybe these were her toys, or her son's toys," Kim added. "And maybe she found them too painful to look at after the men were killed."

"That sounds reasonable," Nicki answered.

"Maybe it wasn't put here at all," Meredith said. "Maybe the trunk washed up here. It could have been taken by the tide from the beach, or it could have fallen off a boat while Dervorgilla was traveling."

"Dervorgilla sold something that helped the family survive," Nicki said, remembering Mrs. Shea's story. "Maybe she found the treasure in this trunk and replaced it with these things. Maybe this was the real treasure chest, and Dervorgilla used it all to save the estate."

Christine sighed. "So there is no treasure now," she said flatly. "And all of our work was for nothing. Instead of having a castle-sized yard sale, Dervorgilla just threw her junk into a trunk and brought it down here. The legend of the fairy treasure is only a story to lure unwary tourists to their deaths."

"We're not going to die," Meredith said firmly, carefully replacing the doll in the trunk. She lowered the lid once again, and tapped it shut.

"Well, what do we do with this stuff?" Laura asked. "Just leave it here?"

"It'll be okay," Kim said. "The trunk is securely fastened, and it's probably too heavy for the tide to carry out through that little opening."

"Kim has a point," Nicki agreed. "The tide—"

"The tide—" Meredith gasped and leaped to her feet. "I forgot about the tide! What time is it?"

"It's seven forty-five," Nicki answered, checking her watch in the light. She gulped and looked at Meredith's wide eyes. "What time does the tide—"

"It's coming back in," Meredith said, collapsing in a heap on the top of the trunk. "We can't get out of here. There's no treasure, only a chest of old toys, and we're going to be in here with it for the next twelve hours or so." She looked around at her friends. "I hope you all can tread water."

Christine chewed on her thumbnail nervously, Kim sat silently with her back to the wall, Laura paced frantically, and Meredith sat on the trunk scratching her head. Nicki glanced at her watch again. Eight-thirty. It had to be dark outside, the Sheas and Mrs. Cushman were probably frantic, and the water was undoubtedly halfway through the lower cave they had entered earlier. They had tried to walk out after Meredith's warning, but had found the water already knee-deep up to the point where the cave walls narrowed.

"If we press on, we'll get lost in the dark," Meredith had warned, her tone deadly serious. "Nicki can't shine the light for us while we're swimming out, and the odds are pretty great that we'll get turned around in the dark and never find our way out through that tiny entrance. If we did, the tide's in, and we'd be bashed against the rocks. We can't risk it. We might as well turn back."

So they had returned to the cavern with the odd-shaped rocks and the chest, and now they sat and listened to the sound of rushing water growing louder and stronger.

"You know, maybe the water won't reach this cavern at all," Nicki suggested. "It's not as wet in here as it was in the other cave, and the walls aren't as smooth. That's a good sign that water doesn't churn around in this cavern like it does in the first cave."

"But it still comes in, doesn't it?" Christine chided. "How far? How do we know what will happen in the middle of the night when the tide's all the way in?"

"We don't know anything for sure," Meredith said, her eyes blazing defensively. "But high tide will be about midnight, and it's going to cover this place. Nicki, shine the flashlight on the wall, please."

Nicki shone the light on the gray-brown stone of the cavern wall. "Move the light higher," Meredith commanded. "Up there, above your head. See that line in the rocks? That's the water line. That's where the water reached this afternoon at high tide, and it'll reach there again tonight. Any way you look at it, we're going to be in over our heads."

Laura began to sniffle, and Nicki felt a lump rise in her throat. "So what do we do?" she whispered, turning the flashlight on Meredith.

"Well, I'm not going to sit around and wait for the water to come in," Meredith said. "We've got to *do* something."

"You're right." Nicki took a deep breath. "We haven't searched this entire cavern," she said evenly. "We ought to give it a try. Maybe there's another way out—after all, Meredith said every cave has an end, and if you think about it, the air is fresher in here than it was in the first cave. There ought to be another opening."

"That is a good idea," Kim said, standing up and brushing sand off her jeans. "Searching for another way out is better than sitting here and waiting for high tide."

"Stop talking about that," Laura said, cringing as she covered her ears. "I'm trying not to think about it. I'm not a good swimmer, and there's no way I can tread water until the tide goes out—"

"I'm not thinking about dying," Christine said, sliding her hands into her pockets. "I really believe God's going to take care of us. He's always taken care of us before, hasn't He?"

"Yeah, He has," Nicki answered, patting Christine on the back. "We'll get out of here, we've just got to figure out how. So why don't we get up and keep moving ahead? We'll see where this cavern ends, but we'd better hang on to one another."

"Why do we have to hold hands?" Christine asked, frowning. "I'm a big girl."

"Because," Nicki answered, snapping the flashlight off, "the flashlight batteries are getting weak, and if we're going to have light, we'd better save it." She groped in the darkness and found Kim's small hand. "Kim, drop that shovel, and Meredith, leave the pick axe behind. Everybody grab somebody else and let's keep moving."

"At least we'll know how to find the chest," Meredith said confidently as she grabbed Laura's hand, "I'll bet the Sheas would love to look through that stuff. We can take the doll and book to the Sheas the next time we come here."

"*If* we get out of here," Laura mumbled, "I'm certainly never coming back."

They made their way slowly in the darkness, step by step through the cavern. Nicki led the way, feeling for the cavern's rough wall with her right hand and holding Kim's hand tightly with her left. At one point in their trek Christine began to sing "The Song That Never Ends," and Meredith urged her to keep it up because they moved more steadily and rhythmically when Christine sang. "Besides, someone might actually hear us," Meredith added when Christine paused to clear her throat. "So keep singing. If you get tired, I'll take over."

Walking in the dark cavern was like stumbling through a dark and crowded movie theater when you've been outside in the blinding glare of the refreshment counter. Nicki could see absolutely nothing, but her eyes played tricks on her and painted glowing pictures of red and green sea monsters in the darkness, like oil paintings on black velvet. When she blinked, the images vanished.

Her feet kept moving in time to Christine's song, left, right, left, right, and after a while the only sounds in the cavern were Christine's thin voice, the rhythmic crunch of ten sneakered feet on rough sand, and a vague roar like that of a sea shell. The air hung low and heavy with the pungent smell of the sea, and Nicki could almost taste salt on her tongue. Once, though, a warm earthy breeze grazed her cheek and she paused, but it left her and she moved on.

Nicki didn't realize that her frantic groping for the cavern wall had scraped her blistered fingers raw until she stumbled into a puddle and put out her hand to catch herself. The salt water stung her fingers and palms, and she cried aloud in dismay and pain.

"Are you all right?" Kim asked, her voice heavy with concern. "I'm sorry I did not catch you."

"It's okay," Nicki said, drying her wet hands on her jeans. "But why don't you just put your hand on my shoulder for a while? I think I need to lead with my left hand for a while."

"Let me lead," Kim offered, stepping into the forward position. "You stand behind and rest."

"How wide is that puddle you hit?" Meredith called from the back of the line.

Nicki fumbled in her jacket pocket and pulled out the flashlight. Turning it on, she shone the beam on the puddle, and her eyes opened wide in horror.

"That's no puddle, that's the ocean," Christine yelled, her scream echoing through the cavern. "We'll never get out this way."

"We haven't gone anywhere," Meredith said. She grabbed the flashlight from Nicki and shone it at a dark object ahead of them in the darkness. There stood the trunk, with Meredith's pick axe propped against it.

"We've gone in a circle?" Nicki asked, the truth slowly descending upon her. "But that couldn't be right. If we had gone in a circle, the entrance should be near here—"

"It is," Meredith said, gesturing at the wall ahead of them, "and it's letting in water now. The tide is coming in, and it looks like this cavern is just one big, round room. I guess there is no other way out."

"There has to be!" Nicki answered, fighting the fear that rose in her throat. "Once as we were walking, I thought I felt a breeze, but I didn't say anything because I wanted to be sure. We've got to go back and find it! I know there's a way out!"

"Maybe this time we could go around with the flashlight on," Kim added. "We know our way in the dark, now let us try the light. Maybe we'll see something we missed."

Nicki nodded. "That means we have to walk in water," she said, turning to Laura and Christine. "It can't be helped."

"I know," Laura said softly. "It's okay, I won't complain."

Nicki nodded. "Okay," she said, slapping her hand on Kim's shoulder. "Everybody grab onto the person in front of you, and let's go around again, this time with light. If you see anything, shout it out."

Christine cleared her throat and began "The Song that Never Ends" again. Meredith groaned. "If I never hear that song again," she told Nicki, "I'll be happy for the rest of my life."

When they reached the chest again, the sea water had risen to knee level, and Nicki was bone-tired. Sloshing through sea water was much harder than simply walking on sand, and Nicki knew none of them had the energy to go around many more times. Besides, if there was no other opening, weren't they just wasting their time and energy?

"You know, we may be going about this the wrong way," Meredith said as they paused to lean against the wall to rest. "We've been around the cavern twice and found nothing. Maybe there's a way out in the center of the room."

"A way out in the center?" Christine asked, her voice rising hysterically. "How can that be? There aren't any walls in the center of the room, so how can we climb out if there's nothing to climb out on?"

"Stop and think," Meredith said. "Be quiet and listen. Nicki, what time is it now?"

Kim shone the weak beam of the flashlight on Nicki's wristwatch. "It's nine-thirty," Nicki answered dully. "Two and a half hours until high tide."

"So it's dark outside," Meredith said, raising an eyebrow. "Kim, turn the flashlight off."

Kim snapped the light off and they stood in darkness for several minutes. As her eyes grew accustomed to the lack of light, Nicki realized she could see vague shadowy outlines of her friends. There wasn't much light, but they were no longer in total darkness.

"Meredith, I see what you mean!" Nicki cried, thrilled. "Somehow, light is coming in here."

"That's right," Meredith nodded. "We didn't see it earlier because the moon hadn't risen. But there's a full moon tonight, and that means light—we just have to find the opening where our moonlight is leaking through."

Nicki looked around. "How do we do that?" she asked. There were no obvious moonbeams, nor could she see anything overhead except blackness.

"Instead of walking around the walls, we need to walk into the center of the room and continue until we hit the other wall," Meredith answered. "While we're walking, everyone look up and search the ceiling for light. If we hit the wall before we find anything, we'll lead off in another direction."

"Couldn't we do this faster if we split up?" Laura asked.

"No!" shouted Meredith, Nicki, Christine, and Kim.

Nicki softened her tone as Laura visibly shrank back. "We don't want to take a chance on being separated," she said. "The water's still rising, and soon we won't even be able to see the chest—our only landmark. We've got to stay together."

"Okay," Laura whispered.

"I'll take the front position this time," Meredith volunteered. "Everybody grab onto someone else and keep a sharp lookout. Christine, as much as I love that song, let's keep it quiet this time, okay? We want to listen for wind, sounds of dripping water, anything unusual."

Christine nodded, and Nicki felt her spirits begin to rise. There had to be a way out, and they had to find it. There wasn't much time left before the hungry waters of the high tide would fill the cavern.

16

Nicki chuckled grimly as the old saying came to her mind. *That's what we are,* she thought as the girls sloshed their way through the murky cavern, *the blind leading the blind. None of us knows where we're going.*

The rough Irish brogue of Molly O'Hara also rang in her memory. "Nobody goes on the western side of the island," Molly had said. "The tide comes in quickly . . . several folks have drowned off the western shore in years past. Me own brother was lost off that beach . . . ."

"Molly's brother was lost off the western beach, do you remember her telling us that?" Nicki asked aloud. "I wonder if he found this cave and never came out."

Laura began to whimper again, and Nicki was sorry she'd said anything. If they began to think escape was impossible, they'd give up, and then they'd never get out. She had to do something to keep the other girls' spirits up.

She was about to suggest that they tell stories when Meredith interrupted her. "Land ho," Meredith called out, exhaustion in her voice. "I've hit rock. And judging from the feel of it, I'd say it's the opposite side of the cave."

"Let me see," Nicki said, fumbling in her jacket pocket for the flashlight. She snapped it on, praying that the weak batteries still had enough energy to muster a beam. "It is the other wall," Nicki muttered, staring at the gray-brown stone. "Now what?"

"We regroup and head out at another angle," Meredith said confidently. "Come on, Christine, give me your hand."

"I'm tired," Christine protested, slapping the water in anger. "The water's up to my waist, it's cold, and I'm too tired to move."

"We can't give up," Kim said softly. "We just can't. We have to keep looking for a way out."

"Maybe there's even another cavern that's higher," Laura suggested. "Maybe we can find that."

Christine sighed and placed her hand in Meredith's. Nicki flicked off the flashlight switch, and they were in darkness again. "Okay, let's move out," Meredith called. "Stay together, everybody."

We must look like a huge blind worm trying to swim upstream, Nicki thought. Even the simplest movements were becoming more difficult as the water inched higher and higher. Once Laura tripped on something and her head slipped beneath the water. Nicki and Kim, who held her hands, yanked her up quickly, but not soon enough to prevent Laura from panic. She came out of the water screaming, and even now she still whimpered softly, her hand trembling in Nicki's.

"Hey!" Meredith's voice echoed sharply through the darkness. "There's something here. Nicki, shine that flashlight, will you?"

Nicki reached into her jacket pocket and her heart sank when she realized the pocket had been underwater. "I don't know if it will work, Meredith, the light's been under water," she said, pressing urgently on the switch. The light flickered, then went out. Nicki felt like crying.

"That's okay," Meredith said, splashing around in the dark. Nicki could see the outline of Meredith's head— was it her imagination, or did Meredith's form seem less shadowy? And wasn't Christine's red hair gleaming in the dark?

"There's more light here," Nicki said, pushing forward and pulling Laura along with her. "What have you found, Meredith?"

"I don't know exactly, but it's a big pile of rocks, and they're covered in good old garden-variety mud, not sand," Meredith said. "The mud is less gritty between my fingers. That means somehow dirt from the land above us has washed down here."

"You mean there's a hole in the roof?" Christine asked, her eyes wide.

"Something like that," Meredith said, her voice relaxed. "There's some kind of opening, for sure."

"Remember when Meredith said it'd be neat if we could pop right up through this cave into Molly's kitchen?" Nicki said, her voice bright. "Maybe we can pop right up into James Murray's garden!"

"There are rocks and boulders here," Meredith said, feeling her way through the darkness. "Sort of like a giant stalagmite, I guess."

"Stalag-what?" Kim asked, moving closer in the water.

"Stalagmite: a deposit of calcium carbonate formed on the floor of a cave by the drop of calcareous water," Meredith recited. "But this hasn't been formed by calcium carbonate, it's been formed by rocks and dripping soil from above us. The rocks are completely different from those in this cave."

"I don't care about that, can we get out?" Christine called. "It's getting really deep, Meredith, and I don't want to even *think* about what could be swimming in here with us."

She had no sooner spoken when a large splash echoed from somewhere else in the darkness of the cavern, and Nicki shivered. "Nicki, that was you splashing, right?" Laura asked in a strangled little girl voice.

"No, Laura, it wasn't," Nicki answered. She glanced toward Meredith. "So can we climb out of here on those rocks?"

"I think so," Meredith said. "If we can't climb all the way out, maybe we can at least get high enough to be above the tide level. I'll start climbing, and I'll talk you all through it."

Meredith pulled herself up onto the first rock, and Nicki heard the sound of water streaming out of her clothes. "Okay, Christine, grab the rock and lift yourself up," Meredith coached. "Then follow my voice."

"I can see you, Christine!" Nicki crowed as Christine climbed higher. "Your hair glows in the dark."

"Very funny," Christine answered, her voice quivering as she struggled to balance herself on the rocks.

Kim began her climb next, and Nicki helped Laura find the rocky niches the other girls had used for footing. As Laura moved up and out of the way, Nicki took her first step up onto the rock and pulled herself out of chest-deep water. As water ran out of her jacket, she sighed in relief.

"How are you doing up there?" Nicki called to Meredith. "Can we get all the way out?"

Meredith's voice seemed to come from a great distance. "Keep coming," she called. "From what I can tell, there's a tower of rocks here tall enough for us to sit on, as long as we sit in a single line. I can see the opening to the surface, but I can't reach it."

"I have a rope, remember?" Christine called out. "Can you throw it through the opening?"

"No, there's nothing for it to catch on," Meredith answered. "But if you keep on coming upward, we can at least be out of the water's way. We ought to be able to ride out the tide, and we can walk out in the morning."

"What if we go to sleep on a rock and fall off this tower of yours?" Laura asked. "Have you thought about that?"

"Who can sleep?" Christine answered. "I don't know about you, but there's no way I can sleep on a ledge with sea monsters and sharks waiting in the water below me."

"Sharks?" Laura's eyes gleamed wide and bright in the darkness. "There are sharks?"

"Could be," Christine answered calmly as she climbed behind Meredith.

Kim laughed. "Laura won't be sleepy now," she said, moving up onto a higher rock.

Nicki followed and felt her knees emerge from the water. "Good going, Christine," she said. "I just hope you were kidding about sharks, because my feet are still in water."

They climbed as high as they could, and then made themselves secure among the rocks. Nicki couldn't see the opening Meredith described, but a warm breeze brushed across her hair like ghostly fingers. Nicki sat up straighter and welcomed it. Fresh air! If fresh air could come in, a way out existed, even if they couldn't reach it.

"I'm sure everyone is looking for us," Nicki said, trying to read the hands of her watch in the gloom. "It's got to be ten-thirty, and Mrs. Cushman must be having a fit."

"We should try calling out for help," Meredith said. "But not too loudly. We don't know how stable this rock tower is, and I'd hate to cause an avalanche."

"I'm trying not to breathe as it is," Christine's voice rang out in the darkness. "My rock doesn't feel very steady. It wiggles."

"Don't jiggle it, then," Meredith cautioned. "I'll call out when I can, then I'll stop and listen. The rest of you ought to save your voices."

So Meredith yelled, and listened, yelled, and listened again. No one answered, not even the wind, and Nicki curled up on her rock and pulled her feet securely under her. She was last in line and the lowest on the rock tower, and though she had managed to pull herself completely out of the water at first, now the encroaching tide had risen higher and water again licked her knees. In another hour, she'd be sitting in water up to her neck at least, and there was no place else to go.

"Hello!" Meredith yelled again, her voice echoing strangely in the cavern. "Help! Can anybody hear me?" Meredith ducked her head as she listened, then snapped her fingers. "I hear something!" she whispered, rising to her knees. She balanced herself precariously on the rock and thrust herself as close as she dared to the opening that yawned out of reach.

"Hello!" Meredith screamed at the top of her lungs. "Can anybody hear me?"

Nicki closed her eyes and prayed that someone was out there. From far away a rhythmic thumping sounded, then Nicki thought she heard the swish of someone running through tall grass.

"Hello?" a man's voice called down, and Nicki felt her heart begin to pound.

"Hello, it's us," Meredith called up toward the opening. "We're trapped down here, but we've got a rope. Can I throw it to you?"

Christine swiftly untied the rope from her belt and passed it to Meredith, who coiled it in her hand. The man called down again, and this time Nicki recognized the voice: Maurice O'Griffin stood on the wonderfully solid earth above them.

"What in heaven's name are you girls doing down there in that hole?" he asked, his rough Irish brogue cutting through the stillness. "Dinna anybody warn you about the dangers of Cravenhill Island?"

"No, but we'd love you to help us out," Meredith said, her voice rising in relief. "We were down here looking for the treasure, you see, but the tide came in and—"

"The treasure?" Maurice's voice hardened. "Did you find it, now?"

Meredith laughed. "Actually, I think we did," she said, giggling in her relief. "In an old trunk down here—"

"I'll be back," Maurice said, pulling away from the hole in the earth. "Dinna you move, just stay put, and I'll be back."

He moved away, and the girls were alone with the rising tide once again.

17

He's not coming back, I tell you," Christine remarked glumly. "Why would he leave us? If he had gone to get help, he'd have been back by now."

"He didn't need help anyway because we had a rope," Nicki pointed out. She was standing again; the water had risen over the rock she had been sitting on and was once again up to her waist. She stretched her tired legs carefully because she didn't want to splash and alarm the other girls. But Laura was standing, too, and Nicki was sure only Kim, Christine, and Meredith were still on dry rock. How high would the water go? The tide still wasn't completely in, and the water would continue to rise for at least another hour.

"You know, I've been thinking," Meredith said, her voice floating down to the others. "Maybe the bad luck of Cravenhill Castle is part coincidence and part invention. Think a minute—when did things really begin to go badly for Trant and his family?"

"When Trant fell out of the tree?" Kim suggested.

"No," Meredith answered. "When the twelfth John Shea died, and the Sheas had to come up with money for the estate taxes. They should have been able to sell a few things and raise the money with no problem. But no one ever answered their ads, and no one even came to visit the castle after it was advertised for sale."

"Why?" Christine wondered aloud.

"Because no one ever knew about the ads," Meredith said, snapping her fingers. "How were the ads placed? Cravenhill Castle doesn't have a telephone, so the ads had to be mailed in. How does the mail get off Cravenhill Island? Maurice O'Griffin takes it to Dingle, where it's posted. If Maurice O'Griffin never took the mail, and never posted it—"

"Then no one would even *know* about the castle's being for sale," Nicki gasped. "And no one ever knew about the art for sale, either."

"Wait a minute," Christine said, "some people knew. Mrs. Shea herself talked to those dealers in London about buying some of the castle's paintings."

"And they came all the way to Dingle to see them," Laura added. "One guy was supposed to come the day we arrived."

"But something in Dingle convinced him not to make the trip over to Cravenhill Island," Meredith pointed out. "Who better to do that than Maurice O'Griffin, who could have refused to take him, or could have told him stories about the art being poor or worthless—"

"He could have told anyone anything," Nicki surmised. "The point is, everything that happened on Cravenhill Island went through Maurice O'Griffin. All communication from the castle is filtered through Maurice O'Griffin and his radio."

"Why would Maurice want to hurt Trant's family?" Kim asked. "I thought he liked the Sheas."

"Greed," Meredith summed it up simply. "He wanted the place for himself. If the Sheas don't raise the money they need by the end of the month, the castle will go up for auction. If Maurice controls all access to the island, it's very likely he'd be the only person to show up to bid. He could get the entire castle and island for next to nothing."

"And remember how Trant told us that Maurice likes bringing tourists over to the castle and charging them five pounds per person?" Christine pointed out. "Trant said Maurice would have the place open for tourists every day if he could."

"And there's always the treasure," Nicki said. "Maurice really thinks we found the famous Shea treasure. He didn't know, Meredith, that you were joking when you told him about the trunk."

"So if he thinks we found the treasure—" Christine's voice faded away, and she sighed. "He's not coming back for us, is he? He doesn't want us to find the treasure for the Sheas. He wants to wait and claim it for himself."

"He's probably telling the others right now that he searched the fields and found nothing," Meredith said. "So no one else will even come along to search this area."

"Well," Laura's voice trembled, "I'm glad we're together. And Meredith, you and Kim and Christine may make it out of here okay, but Nicki and I are almost under water again. So tell my mother I love her, okay? And tell Trant—"

"Hello!" A joyful voice from above surprised them and a bright beam pierced the darkness. Nicki couldn't see who called them from above, but it definitely wasn't Maurice O'Griffin.

"Professor Fulton, is that you?" Meredith cried.

"None other," the voice replied. "I had rather a hunch that you girls might have found a cavern, and judging from the lay of the land I hoped there would be a subterranean opening. Lucky I stumbled upon it."

"Lucky for us!" Nicki cried, squeezing Laura's hand. "Did Maurice O'Griffin tell you where to find us?"

"No, he didn't." The professor's voice was edged with disapproval. "But are you girls okay? Shall I bring you up?"

"Please," Laura cried, shivering again.

"I'll have you out of there straightaway," the professor promised. "I'm setting off a flare—the others will be here to help in a jiffy."

Within moments, a long, strong rope descended through the opening. A bright flashlight shone from the end of the rope, and Meredith grabbed it and focused it downward toward Nicki and Laura. For the first time, Nicki saw how muddy and dirty they all were. Laura, the prettiest and most fashionable girl at Pine Grove Middle School, looked like a muddy Raggedy Ann.

Nicki laughed. "Warm clothes, dry socks, and a warm bath," she said, looking up at the small opening in the dark rock that had surrounded them for so long. "I'll never take them for granted again."

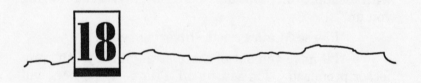

18

"How did you find us?" Nicki asked Professor Fulton when they were all safely upon the solid earth of Cravenhill Island. Mr. and Mrs. Shea, James Murray, and Mrs. Cushman stood with them in the field, surrounding the girls who were now safe and snug in Molly O'Hara's thick cotton towels.

"I was on my way back here to study some unusual rocks when the distress call from Mrs. Shea came over the radio," Professor Fulton explained, his dark eyes shining at Meredith. "Since I was waiting at the dock, I persuaded Maurice to bring me over. I had been searching with the others for an hour or so when I thought about the island's geological structure and found the opening to the cavern. It's so grown over with weeds and grass it's a bloomin' wonder it could be seen at all."

"Maurice O'Griffin found us first," Laura mumbled from the safety of her mother's arms. "But he just went off and left us."

"Where is Maurice?" Mr. Shea asked, looking around. "He didn't come when you lit the flare?"

"I haven't seen him," Professor Fulton answered, shaking his head. "But I suspect he's already left. And if what the girls say is true, I think a bit of playacting might be in order."

"What do you mean?" Nicki asked, her curiosity

stirring.

"Let's let him assume the worst," the professor suggested, "and see what happens in the morning when he comes to pick me up."

"That sounds good," Meredith said, wiping her muddy face with the clean towel Molly handed her. "But for now, can we go inside? I've got a thousand things to ask the professor."

"They can wait," Molly O'Hara said, wrapping a stout arm around Meredith's shoulders. "Am I going to let five muddy girls sit around in wet dirty clothes? Not while there's breath in this body! First a bath and then a cup of cocoa, then you can talk all you like."

"And Trant?" Kim asked shyly.

"He's up and waiting for you, don't you know," Mrs. Shea answered, placing her hand on Kim's cheek. "He said he couldn't sleep until we found you girls."

The clock on the antique mantel struck midnight as the girls sipped hot chocolate around the fire. Nicki realized with a shiver that she would probably be treading water by now if she were still in Cravenhill Cavern. The darkness of the cavern seemed a million miles away from this warm room where family and friends sat enjoying one another's company.

"So, did you find the treasure?" Trant asked, his hand openly squeezing Kim's. "Tell me everything that happened! I wish I could have been there meself!"

"No, you don't," Kim answered. "It was horrible."

"We were approaching this mystery all wrong," Meredith said, putting her mug down on a table. She leaned forward eagerly. "You see, we heard all of Molly's tales about fairies, and we were so carried away by the atmosphere of the castle we didn't stop and think about rational explanations."

"There were no *rational* explanations," Nicki protested. "How many times has a ball of fire chased you through a garden?"

"There is an unusual but sound explanation for that," Professor Fulton said, crossing his legs. "It's called ball lightning, and though it is rare, it does happen. Ball lightning is thought to be plasma, a superheated gas whose atoms have been stripped of their electrons. It's just one of the unusual atmospheric disturbances that I've come to study here on Cravenhill Island."

"A ball of lightning?" Molly said, her face screwed up in confusion. "It's not fairies?"

"No," Meredith said, "not fairies."

"What about the time we saw the fairy fort?" Kim asked. "We actually saw it, Professor, rising up out of the water. A huge city, with castles and trees, just as Molly described it."

"Ah, sure, I wouldn't lie about that," Molly inserted, nodding confidently. "Dinna I tell these girls the truth? I've seen this city meself, at least a dozen times."

"You saw the fata morgana," Professor Fulton nodded. "I saw it myself this morning. It's actually a mirage formed from the images of the rippling sea. Shifting winds ripple the images, causing the vision to oscillate between sea and sky, brightness and darkness, castles and forests. This illusion is common in several unique parts of the world."

"Okay, but what about the time the fairies actually threw things at us?" Laura demanded. "I got hit on the head by a fish!"

"And me," Kim inserted, "I got hit by a big frog."

"I've seen worms fall from heaven," Molly said quietly. "You can't tell me that's normal for anyplace."

"These things happened during a storm, didn't they?" Professor Fulton asked. He waited until the girls and Molly nodded, then he went on. "Often whirlwinds and waterspouts gather up animals from land and sea and transport them in swirling masses until they fall from the sky along with the rain. It was, for the moment, quite literally raining fish, frogs, and worms. Just another of the many charms of Cravenhill Island."

"These things happen in other places?" Molly asked, her eyes wide. "In other parts of the world?"

"Aye, they do," Professor Fulton answered. "And there's a logical scientific explanation for everything." The professor covered a yawn. "And if I could impose upon you, Miss O'Hara, could I be bunking down in one of your comfortable guest rooms? I'm a little tired from all the day's happenings, and I've got to be up and about early in the morning."

"I'll take you upstairs," Molly said, moving toward the hall with her usual dignity. "Anyone who has saved the life of me girls deserves the best room in the house."

"I didn't do so much," the professor said, standing. He winked at Meredith. "It was their singing that led me to them. Without that, I would have never found that opening in the ground."

"Singing?" Nicki looked at Meredith. "We didn't sing. For a while we did, but we stopped. We didn't sing at all for the last hour or so."

A frown settled on the professor's face. "But sure you did," he insisted, "you've just forgotten. You were singing a sweet song, very pretty. You sounded like a wee angel choir."

Nicki felt an electric spark and knew she was

hearing something beyond all logical and rational explanation. They hadn't been singing, she knew. And while fairies didn't exist, angels did, and maybe the professor did hear angel songs that led him to the girls.

She waited until the professor and Molly left the room, then she leaned forward and whispered to Meredith, "So, Meredith, what do you think—is there really a scientific explanation for *everything*?"

Meredith only shook her head.

"We have an idea," Nicki announced to Mr. and Mrs. Shea, Trant, Molly, James, and the professor the next morning while the entire household sat at breakfast.

"If it's about the Cravenhill curse, forget it," James Murray said, turning pink with embarrassment. "I just made that stuff up to try to keep you girls off that dangerous beach. I dinna know you wouldn't scare off from the idea of digging for treasure."

"We have forgotten the curse," Nicki said. "There's a real reason for all your troubles."

"We think Maurice O'Griffin has been stymieing your efforts to raise money for your taxes," Meredith explained. "If you think about it, he's the only one who could do it. He controls everything that goes in and out of this island."

"But Maurice is our friend," Mrs. Shea protested. "We've known him for years!"

"He may be a two-faced friend," Christine said. "Last night he found us and then left us in the cavern without saying anything to anybody. He thinks we found a treasure in there, and all we found was an old trunk that had belonged to Dervorgilla Shea."

"Oh, yeah, and lots of these," Nicki said, pulling the cross-shaped, reddish brown rock out of her pocket. She laughed. "Christine thought we had stumbled onto an ancient burial ground."

"Let me have a look at that," the professor said, pulling the rock to him. He lifted it and examined it carefully.

"What is it?" Meredith said. "Is it important?"

"Very," the professor said, a funny half-smile on his face. "This is most unusual, even for a place like Cravenhill. This is staurolite, a mineral with the strange propensity to form in the shape of a cross." He turned the rock over and over in his hand and marveled at its construction. "In northwest France, these are said to have been dropped from heaven—more commonly, they are called fairy stones."

"Why?" Christine asked.

"They are supposed to be the tears of fairies who wept when they heard about Christ's crucifixion," the professor explained. "But the cruciform shape is caused by the crystals' atomic structure. They are quite valuable—this is quite a find. I think our university's museum would be willing to pay a great deal for this."

The professor looked up at Nicki. "Would you be willing to part with it?"

"It's not mine," Nicki said, opening her hands. "It belongs to Cravenhill Castle. And there are thousands of these rocks down there in the cavern."

The professor whistled. "Really! Thousands?"

"At least," Meredith said, smiling. She turned to Trant and patted his hand. "I guess we really did find the fairies' treasure. If you can sell even a few of those stones, you'll have more than enough to pay the taxes."

"And you won't have to sell the family paintings," Nicki said, glancing out into the hall where Dervorgilla and the other Shea ancestors seemed to smile down upon the group. "And Cravenhill Castle can stay as it always has been."

The thirteenth John Shea leaned his chin upon his hand. "What do you say, Erin?" he asked his wife. "Do we sell the rocks and keep our home?"

"That's what great-great-great-great-grandmother Dervorgilla Shea would do," Mrs. Shea answered, placing her hand tenderly on her husband's arm. "But really, I don't care what we do, as long as you, Trant, Molly, James, and I are together. As long as we're a family, we have all the treasure we need—in each other."

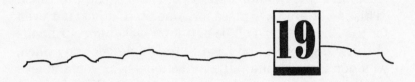

19

A knock sounded on the kitchen door and Molly peeked out through the kitchen curtain. "It's Maurice O'Griffin," she whispered, waving her hands desperately. "Girls, hide yourselves!"

Nicki, Kim, Christine, Meredith, and Laura grabbed their dishes, set them in the sink out of sight, and dashed out of the room. Molly made a distinct effort to calm herself, then she slowly opened the door, her face a mask of sorrow.

"Aye, Molly, I'm sorry about those American girls," Maurice said, his cap in his hand. "Has there been any word from them?"

From her hiding place in the hallway, Nicki peeked into the kitchen through the tiny space between the door and the wall. Molly was giving a performance worthy of an Oscar, and Mr. and Mrs. Shea were playing their parts well, too.

"It's too terrible," Mrs. Cushman said, burying her face in her napkin. "It's so terrible that I've half a mind to buy this place myself just to be near the place where my daughter was lost. I'll move in here with the Sheas, and we'll wait for the girls to show up."

"Even if it takes years," Mrs. Shea deadpanned, patting Mrs. Cushman's hand. "You're welcome at Cravenhill Castle. Why don't you buy it, Virginia?"

Maurice O'Griffin's face turned fiery red. "No, Mrs. Cushman, you wouldn't want to do that," he protested. "This is not a proper place for American ladies, nor even for the Sheas. You'd all be better off washing your hands of this cursed spot and moving to Dingle. Johnny Shea, why don't you let me call the auctioneer for you and let's get things moving? This place has been nothing but sorrow and heartache for the lot of you, don't you know?"

"I couldn't let you do that," Mr. Shea answered, staring steadily into Maurice O'Griffin's eyes. "You've done too much for us all ready, even last night you were out so late searching for our lost girls—"

"I'm nothing but sorry I dinna find them," Maurice answered, swaying sorrowfully on his feet.

"You didn't find even a sign of them?" Mrs. Cushman asked, dabbing at her eyes with her napkin. "You didn't hear a peep or a cry or a call?"

"Nothing, bless you," Maurice answered. He took a handkerchief from his pocket and blew loudly. "Though how I'll ever see a pretty young girl again without thinking of them is beyond me—"

"I can't take any more of this," Nicki said, laughing as the other girls came into the kitchen with her. "You're all excellent actors. Even you, Mr. O'Griffin."

Maurice O'Griffin's jaw dropped and his eyes bulged in astonishment. "By all the saints—" he began.

"Forget it, we've already told them that you found us and left us," Nicki said. "And we know you're the one that's been messing things up for the Sheas. It's all because you want Cravenhill Castle for yourself."

"As a tourist attraction," Laura said, crinkling her nose in distaste. "How tacky!"

"You found us," Christine said, her eyes blazing in her anger. "And you walked off and left us. I wouldn't do that to an animal, but you did it to five helpless girls only half an hour away from drowning!"

Mr. Shea stood up abruptly. "I don't know that you've done anything against the law, but you're no longer welcome on this island," he said, his voice rumbling through the kitchen hall. "We'll hire another boat to ferry us from Dingle, and we'll find another way to post our letters. We've had our lives in your hands too long, Maurice, and we're going to take care of things by ourselves from now on."

Maurice O'Griffin glared at Nicki and her friends. "So you found the treasure?" he snarled, glancing from girl to girl. "Where is it?"

"There," Nicki said, pointing to the staurolite rock on the table. She raised her finger until it pointed at Trant and his family. "And there," she said, her voice softer. "The secret of Cravenhill Castle is that its people are the real treasure. The Sheas are survivors, and you can never steal their spirit, Mr. O'Griffin, no matter how hard you try."

Maurice O'Griffin turned and left the kitchen like a scolded hound, and Molly O'Hara slammed the door behind him with a flourish.

Nicki sat on her suitcase and struggled to close the latches. "I only hope they let us on the plane with all the stuff we've picked up," she said, laughing. "My suitcase is so heavy now!"

"Of course it is, you filled it with rocks," Laura sniffed. "Though why you're taking home those dirty old black sea rocks is beyond me."

"The best kind of souvenir," Nicki answered, smiling. "When things get tough, I'll pick up a rock, smell it, and remember how it felt to wander around in the cold and dark. It will remind me that God brought us out of that pit and that He can do anything!"

"Anything?" Kim asked softly, and Nicki knew from the soft, sad expression on her face that Kim was wondering if she'd ever see Trant again.

"Anything," Nicki whispered, patting Kim on the arm.

"Look!" Christine called, leaning out the window. Above the soft swell of the morning tide, a misty city of towers and castles and turrets glistened between the sea and sky. "The fata morgana," Christine whispered. "I almost forgot how beautiful it is!"

"What a great going-away treat," Meredith said, studying the vision as if she wanted to memorize every detail. "This certainly isn't something we see every day."

"No, it isn't," Kim said, coming to the window. She rested her chin in her cupped hands and smiled at her friends. In a perfect Irish brogue, she quipped, "Did I tell you the story about John Shea and the remarkable treasure on Cravenhill Island?"

"Why, no," Meredith said, mimicking Molly O'Hara's accent. "You say there's a treasure hidden on this island? You wouldn't be fooling me, would you now?"

Kim winked at Nicki. "Ah, sure there is treasure, just not the kind you think. But I'd be here all day long telling you about that!"

About the Author

Angie Hunt lives in Largo, Florida, with her husband Gary, their two children, a Chinese Pug named Ike, and Cassie, a calico cat. She and Gary have been serving in youth ministry since 1977.

Angie recently returned from a trip to Ireland and says that the Irish people are the beautiful country's best feature. "Talkative, charming, and interested," is how she describes the Irish people, "just like the Sheas and Molly O'Hara."

Don't Miss
Any of Nicki Holland's
Exciting Adventures!

#1: The Case of the Mystery Mark

Strange things are happening at Pine Grove Middle School—vandalism, dog-napping, stolen papers, and threatening notes. Is there a connection between the unusual new girl and the mysterious mark that keeps appearing whenever something goes wrong? Nicki and her best friends want to find out before something terrible happens to one of them!

#2: The Case of the Phantom Friend

Nicki and the girls have found a new friend in Lila Greaves. But someone has threatened Mrs. Greaves and now she could lose everything she loves. The girls have one clue that they hope will lead to something to save Mrs. Greaves—if only they can solve the mystery before it's too late!

#3: The Case of the Teenage Terminator

Christine's brother Tommy is in trouble, but he doesn't seem to realize it. Nicki, Meredith, Christine, Kim, and Laura take on an investigation that pits them against a danger they've never faced before—one that could lead to a life-or-death struggle.

#4: The Case of the Terrified Track Star

Pine Grove's track star, Jeremy Newkirk, has always been afraid of dogs, but now somebody is using that information to scare him out of Saturday's important race. Without Jeremy, Pine Grove will never win! Following a trail of mysterious letters and threatening phone calls, Nicki and her friends are in their own race against time to solve the mystery. Can the girls keep Jeremy's worst nightmare from coming true?

#5: The Case of the Counterfeit Cash

Nicki expected fun and sun in the summer before her eighth grade year—not mysterious strangers and counterfeit cash! Nicki, Meredith, Kim, Christine, and Laura are warned to leave the mystery alone. But when Nicki is threatened, she has to solve the mystery to save her own life!

#6: The Case of the Haunting of Lowell Lanes

Nicki and her friends thought it would be fun to help Meredith's uncle at Lowell Lanes for the summer. But then the lights went out and strange things began to happen. Is Lowell Lanes really haunted? Can Nicki and her friends solve the mystery before Mr. Lowell is driven out of business?

#7: The Case of the Birthday Bracelet

Nicki and her friends thought they were taking a nice vacation trip to London, but strange things begin happening even before the girls arrive at their hotel. And when Laura's diamond birthday bracelet disappears, the search leads Nicki and her friends to more danger than they had bargained for!

#8: The Secret of Cravenhill Castle

Nicki and her friends are thrilled when they receive an invitation to spend a few days at a five-hundred-year-old Irish castle. Shrouded in mystery and fairy legend, the castle is everything they expect, and more! The girls must battle the sea, superstition, and their own fears as they undertake a dangerous search for the legendary treasure of Cravenhill Castle.

#9: The Riddle of Baby Rosalind

Nicki and her friends expected a normal flight home from Ireland until Laura meets a woman in the airport and offers to watch her baby. When the woman fails to board the plane with the girls, Laura and Nicki find a note in the baby's diaper bag. Did the mother really abandon the child? Was the woman in the airport really the baby's mother, or was she a kidnapper? Nicki and her friends have only eight hours to find answers to their many questions about the baby in their care.